ARCANE KINGDOM ONLINE

BOOK THREE: THE FALLEN CITY

JAKOB TANNER

Dedicated:

To my mom and dad, who have encouraged and supported me in everything that I've done.

Special Thanks to:

Richard Sashigane for the awesome cover art.

Joseph Gisini for help with the cover typography and design.

Andrew Smith for sage advice.

Everyone who picked up book 1 and 2 (seriously, you're all amazing!)

Thanks to my beta readers and their amazing feedback:

Frank Albelo
Ailsa Bristow
Ezben Gerardo
Jo Hoffacker
Ben Warren

This book wouldn't be what it is today without you guys!

1

The sails of our ship bloomed, propelling us across the sky ocean. The wind whistled over the deck. The crew worked the yards in a hushed silence. Their eyes twitched and their teeth chattered. We were closing in.

The whole world teetered from up top on the crow's nest. The sky was crystal clear. The air was brisk and fresh. Seagulls dipped and dove, catching sky trout with their beaks. I lifted a brass spyglass to my eye to get a closer glance at our target: an enemy supply vessel. The large floating piece of hulking metal housed wares and supplies we desperately needed. Food for the hungry. Medicine for the sick.

Our current mission was to commandeer the ship and take the supplies back to the Laergardian capital of Land's Shield.

The plan, however, was more easily said than done.

There were six fighters on board, patrolling the deck. They were the standard Arethkarian air soldiers: ranging from level 10 to 15, decked head to toe in heavy iron armor. They wore metal helmets with glowing green slits for eyes and air-purifier tusks concealing their mouths. They appeared less than human. Robotic. Tubes of purple mana travelled from their back armor and into their spines. It was special Arethkarian magitech designed to pump mana into their warriors, genetically enhancing their strength and power.

A guard patrolling the deck approached a scrawny and pale crew woman. She was washing the deck, vigorously scrubbing the floor with a small rag and soapy bucket beside her. The guard stopped his patrol, towering over the woman. He arched back his foot and kicked her in the stomach. He pointed to the side, telling her to get out of his way.

I pulled the spyglass down to my chest and shuddered. *Don't worry lady, we're coming.*

I shrunk down the scope and dematerialized it back into my inventory. I jumped out of the crow's nest, grabbing hold of the rigging and descended back down to the deck.

"We ready to go?" I asked, approaching my party.

"Almost ready," said Shade. "But one quick question. Serena here believes she's first mate of this ship, when I would obviously think the honorable position belongs to me. Tell us the truth, *captain*?"

The Lirana, clad in a white tunic and black breeches, turned to me, his pointy cat ears perked up, his eyes wide as possible. He kept a dagger and a pistol on both sides of his waist. His fingers twitched, ready to whip either set out in the event of an undesired answer. Call it a negotiating tactic.

"O captain, my captain," said Serena, shaking her head. She crossed her strong warrior arms and smirked at me. Her long blonde hair fluttered in the wind, while a giant sword was sheathed on her back. "*Tell him.*"

I looked Shade directly into his silver eyes—the same eyes partially glazed over from the three pints he'd already guzzled down that morning, the same persuasive eyes that coupled with his 55 stat points in Luck allowed him to get away with pretty much any cheeky idea he ever considered —and, with a hint of guilt in my stomach, delivered the disappointing news. "Serena's my first mate."

"Hah!" Serena said, snapping her fingers and doing a victory dance in front of the rogue.

"C'mon," said Shade, frowning. "What ever happened to bros before hoes?"

I balked. "Where are you learning this crap?"

A little fox girl in white robes, holding a silver staff, politely raised her hand.

"My bad," said Kari. "He keeps pestering me to learn more phrases of The Chosen."

"What can I say?" said Shade. "It's a pretty great party trick at the pub."

An ostentatious cough cut through the conversation. Our helmsman for hire, a mustachioed mercenary, stood by the ship's steering wheel, grumbling. "Just because the enemy ship isn't picking us up on their radar doesn't mean you can sit around and twiddle your thumbs. I took this job to make money, not to *die*. Are we going to proceed?"

The grumpy NPC navigator was right. We were currently burning as little mana fuel possible to stay afloat, relying on the sails and the wind to keep us moving forward. Standard Illyrian radar detected ships based off mana usage; so as long as you used less than a certain threshold you were undetectable, at least until the enemy spotted you the old-fashioned way.

"Crank the engine and get us close enough to board," I yelled to the helmsman. "It's go time."

The curmudgeonly sky pilot nodded his head and turned away from the wheel and adjusted the levers of the crystal mana engine. The ship shook and sped through the air. The wind whipped our hair back. The motor roared.

"Alright guys," I yelled. "We've done this before. The ship will swoop in and we'll board, taking out the fighters. We have to keep an eye on the turret, making sure none of the crew members play hero and go for a Hail Mary, taking us and the ship with it."

Each of the party members nodded along.

"Lastly, and most importantly, *we stop fighting as soon as the crew surrenders*. We'll let them leave on their escape vessels. We're fighting a battle on two fronts here: the physical war and the mental war. Arethkar has enslaved the players who spawned on its continent out of fear they would harm their way of life. We need to show them The Chosen aren't pure evil. We need to show them we are capable of compassion and empathy like them. Got it?"

Everybody nodded once again. Perfect timing, as the *Horizon's Dream* was flying directly over the supply vessel.

"Now comes the fun part," grinned Serena. She bent over and let Kari get onto her back. "See you two down there."

The warrior ran to the deck and, with Kari clutching onto her shoulders, jumped into the clouds.

"As someone without a double jump ability," Shade yelled over the wind, "I have to say I find this whole process rather unappealing."

I picked up some rope tied around a metal cleat, and handed it to him. "Who needs a special jump skill when you have rope?"

"Says the Aeri who can cushion all of his falls!"

"I got a great new phrase from my world to teach you. Perfect for this very occasion."

"Oh yeah?" he said, his eyebrows raising. "How does it go?"

I walked to the edge of the ship and looked back at my Lirana companion.

"It goes like this—" and, as I jumped off into the sky, I said, "*Don't hate the player, hate the game.*"

I dove through the clouds, the wind lashing against my freefalling body. I barrel flipped so I was falling feet first. Next I channeled my mana towards the bottom of my feet. At first I was falling so fast, the ability was unable to fully break the fall, but it did lessen the intensity. I was gliding more than descending to my demise.

Serena and Kari landed on the deck with a loud thud, kick starting the battle beneath my feet. Soldiers yelled. Rifles fired.

I created a puddle of mana under the soles of my boots, forming a strong enough platform for me to break my fall and jump again. I created a stairway of mana platforms until I landed on the deck.

I was greeted with a beam of light shooting past my head. It was a soldier across the deck. Serena lifted her leg and pounded her foot into the chest of the soldier, pushing him back. The warrior regained his balance and rushed at her with his battle axe. With both hands gripped tightly on the hilt of her massive sword, she thrust the blade forward denting the soldier's metal plating and taking a wallop of points off his HP.

Another warrior came at her from the opposite end and Serena swung her sword, triggering her favorite ability, blade tornado. Spinning on one foot, she rapidly swirled her sword, becoming an indecipherable and deadly blur, protecting herself from any incoming melee attacks. She did more than simply defend herself: the spinning blade cut through the throats of the two warriors coming at her on either side. They collapsed to the floor at her feet.

"Aieeeee!"

Right on cue, Shade swung from his rope overhead, dropkicking a guard on the ship's sentry tower as he landed. He pulled out both his daggers and ferociously dug his knives back and forth into the warrior's back with the same intensity of a professional masseuse. He was providing stress relief through destruction.

The thief twirled his knives and sheathed them at his sides. He crouched down on the stairwell of the control tower and pulled out his guns, blocking the enemy crew's ability to call for reinforcements. Shade fired off pistol rounds from his higher position, offering support from a distance.

Two soldiers ran at me with bayonets. I stretched out my arms and opened my hands. I unleashed ice wave: two frozen shards flung through the air and knocked the soldiers back. A crippling frost crackled up their legs, stiffening their bodies as they moved forward.

I slid across the deck with my flame dodge ability: thrusting myself back, leaving a blazing line of fire at my feet. Next my hands heated up. Two molten fireballs formed in either palm. I whipped them across the deck at the frosted soldiers. Two headshots. The warriors lifted up their hands to their metal helmets, smoke pouring out of their eye slits. They collapsed to their knees, screaming in pain. I whipped more fireballs at them, watching the burning debuff stack beneath their status bars, eating away at their HP until they were finished.

+105 EXP!

+105 EXP!

"Is that it?" I asked.

A soldier poked his head out from behind a group of barrels with his finger on the trigger of a rifle. He pulled it. The laser blast came straight towards me. I clenched my fists, triggering my stone skin ability, but the spell's cast time wasn't quick enough. I was about to get a burning hole right through my chest, but the excruciating pain didn't come. A golden glow washed over me instead. The laser smashed into my chest and I stumbled back. The hit to my HP wasn't dramatic.

"You're welcome," said Kari, from across the deck, holding up a cute peace sign with her fox fingers.

Serena ran towards the final soldier, blade raised. He screamed, "I surrender!"

She stopped and pointed her sword over the Arethkarian warrior, ready to strike his neck at a moment's notice.

"I think that's all the soldiers covered," I said, walking over to Serena and the fallen warrior. "Where's the crew?"

"They're below."

"Good. Now get up."

We found the crew operators, sky pilot, and laborers all below deck. The cleaning woman from earlier was also there. She looked as terrified as she had been when facing the Arethkarian soldier above deck. They were all this way, solemn and fearful. As players with the ability to come back to life after death, we were practically demons to them. Letting them go would be the first step in making them see us as the opposite to the tyrannical monsters their kingdom made us out to be.

"We're not going to hurt you," I said. "We're taking this ship and its supplies back to our kingdom, but we'll let you guys leave on your escape ships."

The crewmen nodded hesitantly.

"I'm serious," I said. "We're letting you go."

We guided the crew of about fifteen onto two different escape ships. They huddled and squeezed into the tight platforms. I slammed the door and gave them a thumbs up. Their engines rumbled and they puttered out into the sky.

I turned to congratulate my team for a job well-done when something shuffled behind me. An Arethkarian soldier appeared out of nowhere. He must have been hiding on the other end. He leapt through the air with two knives, ready to backstab Serena.

Lightning shot forth from my palm, wrapping a paralyzing cage around the attacker. I ran up to him and charged a fireball in my hand and formed a flaming fist. I cocked back my arm and punched the fighter until he was at the edge of the ship. Then I kicked him off. His screams fading into the endless sky.

I took a deep breath and turned back to the crew. They looked at me with pale, solemn faces.

Serena crossed her arms against her chest. "So much for compassion, huh?"

She caught my eye and I looked to the floor. "I had to make a quick decision. You or him. I chose *you*."

She was about to reply when a shadowy metal airship emerged from the clouds heading straight for us.

"Oh crap," said Shade.

It was exactly what we were hoping wouldn't show up.

Reinforcements.

2

A giant dreadnought flew towards us in the sky. The menacing ship was overloaded with offensive weaponry: gun towers across the deck, turrets lining the edges, and cannon holes dotting across the massive metallic hull. Tendrils of black smoke spiraled around the enemy ships as well. *Shadow Wraiths.* They were horrifying creatures formed of black shadow and glowing red eyes. Monsters the Arethkarian armada used as foot soldiers and cannon fodder. They weren't normal game monsters either; they were players equipped with horrible necklaces full of passive debuffs like enslavement and demonic transformation.

"Serena," I said. "Go to the navigation quarters and take control of the vessel. Everybody else, it's time to cause a distraction."

Right on cue, the *Horizon's Dream* puffed out of the clouds and emerged right beside the Arethkarian supply vessel. The mustachioed helmsman was less than pleased. "You told me we were doing light privateer work, not fighting the Arethkarian armada on our bloody own!"

There was no time to argue with him so I shrugged. "Shit happens."

He grumbled and turned back to the steering wheel, keeping his eye on the approaching enemy ships.

Shade and Kari hopped across the deck of the supply vessel and back onto our ship. I took one last glance over to Serena. She looked up from the mana engine and gave me a thumbs up.

I ran across the deck at full speed, jumping onto the metal rails first, then jumping again across the small but deadly gap of air between our two ships. I landed on the deck of the *Horizon's Dream*. I stumbled and was about to face plant into a barrel when Shade caught my arm.

"Close one," said Shade, pulling me back to my feet and helping me regain my balance. "To think you may have fallen and hurt yourself before our big battle. It's a good thing you have someone like me around to stop you from making—"

"Dude, this doesn't make you first mate."

The Lirana shook his head and crossed his arms. "I should've let you bloody fall."

Something pulled at my leg. Kari tugged on my trousers, looking up at me with her big hazel fox eyes. "What's the plan, boss?"

The engine of the supply vessel roared and headed through the sky towards Land's Shield. We needed to delay the current Arethkarian interception until Serena and the supplies were back at HQ, nice and safe. That meant a fight. Not one we hoped to win, merely one we wanted to prolong.

"Reef the sails," I yelled to the ship's hired NPC crew. The group of men and women rolled up the sails of the ship, decreasing our natural wind speed but increasing our maneuverability.

One crew woman ran up to me from across the deck. "Captain—there's an incoming holo-transmission from the enemy ship. Do you want to take it?"

If it meant talking with Arethkarian slave masters, *not really*, but communication even with enemies was better than barreling straight into a shoot-out.

"I'll take it in the captain's quarters," I said. "Shade, Kari —look after the crew, make sure the preparations for battle are in place."

I strode across the deck, sky sailors running around me as they tied up the sails and prepared the turrets at the side of the ship. The helmsman shook his head as I approached the entrance to the captain's quarters.

"We need to retreat this instant," he said.

"I agree. Let's wait ten more minutes."

The helmsman went red in the face. I continued towards my office.

The captain's quarters of the *Horizon's Dream* was the most ornate and beautiful room on the ship. Two walls divided by clear glass windows, angled upward to meet the bottom of the quarter deck. One wall was taken up by a giant painted map of Illyria, showcasing the five major continents of the world and the treacherous cloud oceans between them. Beneath it was a chest, full of wine bottles I'd been meaning to move to the crew's living quarters. On the other side was a wall with an orange manalit sconce, a green banner featuring the Laergardian heraldry, and a bed resting below. I had yet to sleep in here as none of our mission's had been overnight affairs.

Bringing the room together was a large wooden desk standing on top a vibrant red Persian carpet, which to be fair, wasn't an actual Persian carpet but one imported from the continent of *Solmini*, but the design was quite similar.

A soft hum came from a crystal candelabra on the desk. It was a holo-transmission device. I pressed it and a translucent screen appeared in front of me, followed by a moving image of a bald man with a black goatee and faded gray eyes, staring outward in a serious manner. Weird orange veins crawled up from the side of his neck. They were inhuman but I didn't know what it was and the screen cut the rest of the man's body from me.

"Please confirm you are the captain of the Laergardian frigate, *Horizon's Dream*, floating in the eastern quadrant of Argon's Rage."

Ugh. Arethkarian generals were known for speaking in this manner. Bureaucratic and robotic. They liked to place a veneer of order over everything they took part in, including blowing an enemy ship out of the sky.

"This is the captain. Who the hell are you?"

"I am Sir Oren Kaige, commander of the Arethkarian fleet, tasked with conquering Land's Shield and the wider Laergardian continent."

"Cool beans," I said. "*What do you want?*"

"You've recently boarded a supply vessel belonging to our fleet. If you do not return it to our possession, we'll be forced to blow both you and it out of the sky."

"Really? You'll be *forced* to? Forced in the same way you've enslaved The Chosen?"

The general winced at me, disgusted by my gall.

"Let's be real here," I continued. "You've found a lone Laergardian ship—you'd blow us up regardless of whether we'd stolen your vessel or not."

The general's eyes locked onto mine. "Spin words about me however you wish, but nothing will stop me from doing what's necessary to protect my family and fellow Arethkarians from the tyranny of The Chosen. Prepare to be boarded."

The holo-transmission shut off and a massive tremor shook the ship, rattling the wine bottles in the crate. Yells and screams came from above.

I opened the door to the above deck. Echoes of lasers and cannonballs cut through the wind. I hurried up the steps. Beams of light rushed overtop the surface of the deck, barely missing us. Our mustachioed helmsman spun the wheel and cranked the engine, dodging two more cannonballs flying straight for our hull.

A large echo came from the dreadnought as three new cannon blasts came hurling towards us. This attack was different somehow. The cannon balls burned shadowy black smoke, leaving tendrils of dark magic as they rocketed in the direction of our ship.

The helmsman turned the ship and moved downward in the sky. The cannons chased after us like homing missiles. The fiery projectiles came closer and closer. I shut my eyes and braced for impact.

The incoming cannon blasts burst into a cloud of dark smoke. The wisps of shadow took on the contours of a monster. Red eyes glowed through the dark mass. A shining blue necklace stuck out between the head and the rest of the body. *Shadow Wraiths*, I thought, except they were something else. The shadows quickly took a more humanoid shape, forming arms and legs. The wisps of ethereal smoke hardened and turned into a chitinous outer layer: morphing the shadow wraiths into malnourished devils. Their teeth were sharp vampiric razor blades. Their fingers were spiked claws. They back flipped through the air and dug their nails into the wood of the main mast. They spun around the pole and rapidly crawled down, screeching as they came towards us.

Shadow Crawler
Level 13
HP: 460
MP: 14

A wave of lasers rushed across our deck, slicing through the sails. Another set of blasts knocked into the wood of our hull. *Shit.* This was not going well.

"Everyone stay at your stations," I yelled. "Those on turrets—shoot defensively, negate as much incoming fire as you can." I turned to the helmsman. "Keep us moving. We need to dodge as many attacks they send us as possible."

I ran to the center of the deck, next to Shade and Kari. "Time to take these guys out."

The shadow crawlers descended towards us, swinging from the masts. I flicked my fingers and conjured a ball of flame in my palms. I arched back my arm like a baseball pitcher, cranking it further and further back. With all my strength I shot the flame ball towards the demonic shadow. The molten orb flew through the air. The shadow crawler exploded in a cloud of smoke; my flaming projectile smashed into the airship instead. The shadow crawler exploded back into existence right in front of my face. My eyes bulged with shock. The creature took the opportunity to dig its clawed hands into my stomach, taking out a third of my HP with the surprise attack. My whole body went cold. Blood leaked out my stomach. White noise echoed through my ears. I lost balance and tumbled backwards.

Shade kicked the crawler in the gut and then fired off a pistol round at it. The creature stumbled across the deck.

The thief let off another round, but the creature regained its footing and dodged the attack.

"Hope this helps, Clay," yelled Kari, lifting her small staff in the air. Silver light emerged atop her head. Next a golden glow surrounded my entire body. First my open stomach sealed itself up, then the scars and wounds faded away. My HP shot back up to full.

Healers—even if you never wanted to play one, you loved anyone who did.

"These crawlers are too fast," I said. "We need to slow them down, but I can't hit them."

I flicked my hands open and let a burst of lightning shoot across the deck into Shade's feet, granting him *shocking speed*. I quickly threw the spell out to Kari and then myself.

"Try this Clay," said Kari, shooting out another beam of warm light towards me. My body relaxed and my senses heightened. I followed the shadow crawlers' movements now with sharper perception. A message ran across my HUD.

Keen Sight (Buff): 15% better accuracy and perceptiveness. Hope this is what helps you survive, nerd (Duration: 2 minutes)

A crackling whip of lightning shot out from my palm, slithering across the deck like a snake. It slammed into one of the shadow crawlers, wrapping its thorny electric vines all around the creature until it was paralyzed with lightning cage. I wanted to ensure the creature stayed slow so I ran up to him and, with both my arms stretched out, launched ice wave, freezing his already paralyzed body.

Shade came in from behind, leaping through the air

with both his daggers drawn. They slammed into the back of the shadow crawler, chipping through the hardened skin and into its smoky flesh. The thief wasted no time, following his backstab instantaneously with another move. Twirling blades. He spun around with his two daggers and then jumped in the air doing an uppercut slash. The chipped bits of demonic skin flew across the deck.

I threw fireballs in for support while Kari did the same, using one of her few offensive spells: holy stone. A burst of magical white rock smashed into the shadow crawler.

The creature's HP fell to 5%. The hardened layer of skin crumbled and fell onto the deck of the ship into a pile of ash. The creature returned to a cloud of smoke with glowing red eyes. The necklace glimmered. The demonic cloud of smoke shot forth across the deck and through the clouds, flinging back towards the enemy dreadnought.

Only two more to go.

The ship trembled and swerved, half the crew fell over. Barrels rolled across the deck. A large cracking sound echoed from below. The hull was hit. Lasers shot across the sky.

"We can't sustain any more damage," yelled the helmsman.

The two remaining shadow crawlers were causing havoc across the ship. They ripped sails and attacked the crew. The acrobatic demons flashed in and out, barely staying in one place for long. There was no rhyme or reason to their movements. It was sheer chaos.

"Shade," I yelled. "Follow my lead."

We ran across the deck towards one of the shadow crawlers. It puffed into smoke. I turned around. *Oh no.*

Across the deck, the crawlers double-teamed Kari. They dug their pincer claws into her little fox body. One going through her stomach, the other digging into her back. Her whole body froze, her face pale with shock.

I flicked the fingers of both my hands, letting balls of molten flame form in my palms. I was a dual-wielding fire machine and these shadow crawlers were my targets. I whipped my fireballs at them. The crawlers exploded into black puffs of smoke, leaving Kari to take the impact of my fireblast.

Shade slid across the deck, scooping Kari up right as my flame balls descended the area.

"You're supposed to protect the healer, not kill her," said Shade. "Forget being first mate, make me bloody captain of this enterprise."

With less than 30% HP, Kari lifted up her weakened arms and cured her body back into the green.

"Stick to the plan guys," I said. "How many more hits can you manage Kari?"

"A few more but not many," she said. "I can keep healing myself but then what about you guys?"

"Don't worry about us," I said. "Buff me again with keen sight and I will be able to stop these things."

A shrill shriek echoed across the sky. The shadow crawler was falling from the top sail, unleashing a leap attack.

Crap.

I clenched my fists and triggered my stone skin spell. The earth spell would cover me in a layer of hardened stone, diminishing the amount of damage I took. The shadow crawler fell towards me. A cannonball rushed through the air, slamming right into the creature's stomach, barreling the creature out into the sky and beyond.

One more remained.

Kari rebuffed me with keen sight and I tracked the final

shadow crawler, running across the deck. I threw out my arms and let lightning burst from my palms towards the creature. The purple electricity wrapped itself around the monster, paralyzing it. I rushed forward and unleashed ice wave next. The debuffs stacked below its health bar. Shade came from behind, pummeling his daggers into its back, chipping away at its health and hardened layer of skin. Kari sent bright white rocks of holy magic flying across the deck, smashing into the paralyzed creature.

Right as the creature hit 5% HP, I dove towards it, gripping onto the metal necklace, the source of its power. I pulled at it with all my strength. It barely budged.

"Why won't you come off?"

The human player beneath the shadow crawler flickered into view. It was a woman. She was pale, bald, and bone skinny. She had a birthmark to the left of her nose.

"*It won't come off...*" she cried. "*Please kill me... Don't make me go back...*"

I shook my head. Tears formed in my eyes.

"No," I said. "I refuse. I won't. Just hang on. We'll figure out a way to get you here. Please—keep hanging on."

The necklace burned my fingers. My HP rapidly depleted. I let go in defeat and the shadowy tendrils covered the player's body, morphing her back into the shadow crawler. The creature flung off the deck and back into the clouds, soaring towards the main Arethkarian vessel.

A message came into my HUD. I crouched to my knees as a wave of mana bullet flew past.

Personal Message: Safe and Sound

Clay! I'm closing in on Land's Shield. You're free to get out

of there. I've also received a message from the king. He
wants to have a meeting with us immediately.

Serena

I turned to the helmsman. "I got the okay from Serena. Turn around and let's get the hell out of here."

"We got one problem," yelled the sky pilot, gripping tightly onto the ship's steering wheel. "While dodging all the attacks, we circled the dreadnought, so now it stands between us and Land's Shield."

"Can we go around it?"

"Not without taking a ton of hits," said the grumpy pilot. He looked at the smoke billowing out from the hull. "I don't know if you've noticed but the ship's kind of on its last legs."

"Why don't we fly underneath it?"

"You mean fly directly at it?" balked the sky pilot.

"Yeah, but below it."

"If we survive," said the pilot. "Please formally accept my resignation."

"Let's talk about this later," I said. "For now, let's get outta here."

The pilot waddled over to the mana engine and turned the usage up to max. The ship thrummed and vibrated with energy, shooting us forward. The NPC navigator gripped the wheel and angled us in the direction of the massive dreadnought. We zoomed right towards a new wave of laser blasts.

"Dive!"

We angled deep into the sky, falling beneath the dreadnought's shadow.

I materialized my spyglass. I squinted and analyzed the ship from its metal plating to its porthole windows, desperately seeking an insight into the shadow wraith technology.

Where did they fly back to when they retreated? The ship's balcony came into view. The bald headed commander—Sir Oren Kaige—looked down towards us. Orange veins throbbed across his neck and continued towards his shoulder and arm. I gagged. Where there should have been a human wrist and hand was a hardened pale green pincer.

My stomach lurched. *No way. I didn't believe it.* In my first hours of entering this VR world, I had fought a corrupted rat creature with unreadable stats, constructed from random bones and inverted flesh. An amalgam of different monster parts all rolled into one. A bit too similar to the enemy general above us.

This was bad.

It wasn't just the king who now desperately needed a meeting.

Arethkar was manipulating the power of the corrupted fragments.

Our enemies had gained control of the game's glitches.

3

We stepped into the king's throne room, our armor and clothing torn and ragged. The chamber was a long hallway with high ceilings, lined with green Laergardian banners hanging from stone pillars, beneath sconces glowing a faint purple mana glow. Large glass windows laid on either side of the room. Between their mullions, Land's Shield was in its late morning throng: chimneys oozing smoke, air trams rushing from one district to the next, builders hammering against the scaffolding of old buildings being repaired and new ones being constructed. The metropolis never slowed down, even as war haunted its fringes.

At the end of the hall, above a stone podium rested the golden throne. From the very back, the king was nothing but a speck. King Fergus sat with a gloomy posture: his shoulders slouching, his nose and mouth resting in his clutched hands. He was thinking, pondering over all the details of his city, country, and the enemies who wanted to destroy it. A lot rested on his shoulders. More responsibility than any one person should have, let alone a fourteen year old.

Behind him stood two knights in the throes of a bitter argument. They were the king's right hand advisors. One knight—Sir Archades—never took off his golden armor and his wolf-like helmet in the company of others. No one knew what his face looked like; how heavily scarred and monstrous it was, fighting wars on the behalf of Laergardian kings. The other knight—Sir Edward—had long brown hair and one faded scar running across his left eye. The two were calculating, powerful warriors and struggled to comprehend the king's faith and trust in both me and my party.

"They're a band of trouble makers," said Sir Archades. "Scoundrels who utilize dark forbidden magic. It's a disgrace to let them fly around with the king's banners on their ship. For this next quest, we must consider Sir Gerald and his sky knights. They're the right people for the job."

"Sir Gerald?" Silver balked.

Nice. Silver was coming to our defense.

"I mean, I agree with you about Clay and his party. They're not worth our time in this discussion, but Sir Gerald is an old fogey now. We must rely on a younger more proven crew."

Never mind.

"Please keep it down," said Fergus as we approached. "This is no way to welcome our guests."

The two knights straightened their posture and fell silent behind the king.

"King Fergus," I said, "I know you called this meeting but I've discovered new information we must address first."

The king nodded, giving me room to speak.

"Sir Oren Kaige. The general leading the Arethkarian armada. He has the arm of a monster. A crab pincer artificially bound to his body. The last time I saw such a weird amalgam of creatures was when we fought the corrupted fragments."

The room fell silent.

"*Pathetic*," spat Edward Silver. "I never had much respect for Arethkar and now they've stooped so low as to use forbidden magic to help carry out their terrible deeds."

"It's *bad*," I said. "They're somehow manipulating the power of the corrupted fragments to their own will.

The king pulled his head away from his hands. He sighed, resting his head against his throne. I got the feeling I wasn't bringing him news he hadn't heard already.

"You knew already?" said Serena, irritated.

The king was about to say more when stumbling out from the side of the room was a large Rorn with a grumpy face and long gray beard. The stout wizard was Theobold Longstaff. He and I went back to my early days in Arcane Kingdom Online. He had helped me unlock my apprentice mage class and upon being corrupted by the evil corrupted fragments and gaining the power of the Prophetic Seal, he was first one to inform me of its power. While under the guise of an NPC, he was actually an early TriCorp developer trapped in the game. He used to reside in Arondale, south of Land's Shield, but after the fiasco with the last court wizard and advisor, Theobold had been hired to replace him.

"I've done it," he said, holding up a golden orb. "Everyone—take a look at my newest inventi—Agh!"

A small explosion erupted in front of the old wizard's face, covering his glasses and bulbous nose in a thin layer of soot and ash. He spit out debris and shook his head.

"Ah, my new court magician," said Fergus, smiling. "I'm happy you came to join us. We were about to get underway."

Theobold nodded. "Please, your majesty, don't mind me."

The king nodded and turned to Serena. "Only recently have I been made aware of Arethkar's potential manipulation of the corrupted fragments. Believe me when I say, I haven't had this information much longer than you have." He sighed and turned to me. "As you already know, Arethkar is waging a war of attrition. They've created trade embargoes and are policing the coasts of both our neighboring continents Renzar and Solmini. While as a continent, we can sustain ourselves for a long time, without trade it means our supplies get limited, prices go up, competition gets fiercer, and those living across the land grow embittered with my rule. Will the people eventually welcome Arethkar with open arms? I doubt it. Will other nobles across the land claim they'll do a better job then me? Certainly. That's exactly where our enemy wants us: fighting amongst each other."

"So what is there to be done?" I said.

"Well, it's clearly only a matter of time before Arethkar wins its war of attrition against us, which means, we must change our tactics."

Sir Archades stepped forward, holding a scroll in his hand. He stretched it out and held it up. It was an old stained map of Argon's Rage, the largest cloud ocean in Illyria, the one separating us with Arethkar. The map had markings for different wind currents, locations of unique sky species, floating islands, and trade routes.

"If you look at this map closely," said Fergus, pointing at it from his throne. "You'll notice a peculiar label on the map. In the upper right corner."

I stepped up and examined the map of the cloud ocean, particularly where Fergus had told me to look. It took me a moment to spot it. A small dot with delicate handwriting above it. The word resting over the dot was one I'd had heard before. *Ariellum*. The lost city of the Lirana.

"But this is—"

"Arethkar is growing more and more powerful," continued the king. "They've learned how to manipulate corrupted fragments and use the power to their own benefit. Our only hope lies in retrieving an ancient device of incredible power: the Ultriga Weapon, last seen in the fallen city of Ariellum."

A quest prompt appeared in my vision.

New Quest Alert: Ariellum and the Ultriga Weapon

The royal king of Laergard, Fergus Ravenmour, wants you to seek out the ancient Lirana capital of Ariellum and uncover the lost power of the Ultriga Weapon.

Quest Type: Unique, Dynamic
Quest Difficulty: Hard
Time Limit: 4 Days
Reward: 25,000 EXP + ?
Accept: Yes/No?

Interesting. The last quest given to me by the former king of Laergard pretty much forced me to take it or face a lifetime imprisoned in a dungeon cell. This quest didn't even come with a failure detail, meaning there were no immediate consequences to declining it. Fergus wasn't going to arrest me or chop my head off if I said no to this mission. Of course, there were still ramifications. They were far reaching, unseen in a future unknown: a dreary world where Arethkar's red banners hung across Land's Shield and all of us players lived in cages with slave necklaces wrapped around our throats. Any desire to escape or fight back would be completely drained from our bodies. We'd be nothing but empty shells.

"Why us?"

"*Exactly the question we were asking,*" said Sir Archades.

"While there may be sky ships with high level captains and stronger crews," said Fergus, "You're the only ship with the power of the Prophetic Seal."

He was referencing the black mark on my wrist, a tainted scar left by the corrupted fragment I had fought in my early days of A.K.O. It was a power created by the game's developers to manipulate the game's code from inside the game. So far it had been a giant curse more than anything else.

"I can explain further," said Theobold, turning to me and waving his hands. "Ariellum was supposed to be the first bit of downloadable content after the game went live and received its first patch. The location is locked behind a special gateway. Only someone with your power can unlock it."

"Downloadable content?" I asked. "Like end-game content? We're not nearly high enough level."

Theobold shook his head. "Not in this case. The Ariellum area was planned to open up after a few weeks of the game's launch. We predicted most players wouldn't have been at max level at that point, so it was content geared more for those around level 20 and above."

Shade stepped forward, cutting the conversation off. He muttered words under his breath and shook his head. "You all know me: I don't take issue with a lot of things. Thievery? I love it. Drinking? I'm always game. Treasure hunting? I'm your man. But *this*—this isn't right. Ariellum fell thousands of years ago. It no longer exists. Whatever lies at the coordinates of the map isn't worth searching for. The Ultriga Weapon destroyed Ariellum. It was the hubris of my people. We shouldn't seek it out unless we wish to seek our own demise."

The thief scratched the back of his head. "You're the boss Clay, but you know where I stand on this. I'll be waiting outside."

The Lirana walked out of the throne room, tail still and forlorn.

Serena crossed her arms. "If what Shade says is true, do we really want to unleash such a power onto the world again?"

"I've discussed it over with my advisors," said Fergus. "We see no other option."

"Didn't the last king on the throne use ancient power in the name of protecting his kingdom?" asked Serena. "How did that end up?"

The throne room went silent.

"Surely this is different," said Edward Silver.

"*I don't have a problem with this quest*," said Kari, waving her hand. "I used to work as a trainee doctor in London. You learn sometimes doing the right thing can be a messy, even gross job. This one time I had a patient who had a toothbrush shoved all the way up—"

"*We get it*," said Serena.

"Basically, I'll go where you guys go," said Kari, with a chipper sound to her voice. "I can't let you go off on adventures without a dedicated healer. Remind me how you guys even survived until you met me?"

I scratched the back of my head, nervously. "Uh, we didn't really."

King Fergus coughed and turned to me. We had heard everyone else's opinion, but now he wanted to hear mine. I was the elected captain of our airship and the de facto leader of the group. I held the final opinion on what our party did and didn't do. I was already learning it was a position I didn't like very much: the decision-maker. A position that was becoming all the more difficult in the field of war. How far was I willing to go to protect those I loved?

I took a breath and closed my eyes. When I opened them, everyone was motionless, frozen, like a movie on pause.

Lounging in the lap of the king was a little girl with brown hair and pigtails.

The ghost girl from my dreams.

4

_____

The girl dangled her feet off of King Fergus, nestling her head into his frozen arms. She wore overalls like a tomboy. Her whole body glowed with a silver ghostly hue. She was a translucent specter. She was filled in enough so she wasn't see-through, but she still possessed an immaterial quality. I had a deep urge to see what happened if I swiped my arm through her stomach. I also had a deeper urge to do nothing because she absolutely terrified me. This girl had been haunting my life in A.K.O. since very early on but this may have been the craziest shit she'd ever pulled.

"What are you doing here? Dreams are more your thing, aren't they?"

"You've noticed the pattern then," she smiled. She picked herself up and slid off King Fergus' leg and walked towards me. "I am the guardian of dreams and dreams are my domain. You blinked—a momentary second of respite. Arguably a miniature dream."

"Sounds like a bit of a stretch—"

"Let's just say I used a lot of power and energy to emerge

here and now, rather than wait for you to fall asleep more potently."

"You're awfully talkative today?" I said. Usually she confronted me quite quickly with only the vaguest of information. This had been the most I'd ever heard her say. "Mind telling me what's so urgent?"

The girl shook her head and sighed. "This quest. Everything that is happening. I don't like it. I'm unsure of its source. Arethkar's manipulation of the corrupted fragments worries me. It means my family members—the other guardians—are helping them. I suspect my father and my sister. I don't know yet. This is a very important warning, Clay. Take the quest but be very very careful. I predict dangerous times ahead."

I was about to ask her what the hell she was going on about but King Fergus tilted his head at me. "Clay—your thoughts on the quest?"

I shook my head and walked to the end of the throne room. "I need time to think."

I walked out to the city, taking the heavy choice along with me.

5

The streets of Land's Shield thronged with activity. I hurried past kids playing soccer in an alleyway and acolytes of the Haeren Church of the Nine helping out the homeless. Air trams and ships swooshed far above the city's rooftops. I passed by a sushi restaurant opened by a Japanese couple who had entered the game together. It was one of the first real businesses started by The Chosen. They had worked diligently on leveling their fishing, skyfishing, and culinary craft skills to the point where they were able to open a business. Their skycrab tempura had become particularly popular with the local NPCs. During one of the few nights off we had from adventuring and doing missions for the king, Serena and I had gone on a date here. Our first in A.K.O.—unless you count saving Arondale from a giant dinosaur or defeating an evil king as romantic excursions.

The restaurant had inspired other player-owned businesses and the area beside the engineering district had become known as Chosen-Town. Other players had opened up hardware stores, while others had created a newspaper called the Land's Shield Times. They had interviewed me quickly for a story about fighting Bertwald and the former King Jared. I only answered questions briefly. Players and NPCs glanced at me as I walked through the streets, recognizing me either from the article or from popular rumors and gossip. My party and I had begun to gain a reputation throughout Laergard. We weren't the strongest or the highest leveled but we were seen as the go-to party when it came to story-driven quests and universal world events.

I turned a corner and entered the engineering district. The air grew heavier with smoke. Machine drilling and buzz saws echoed through the streets. Bright beams of ash flew out of open warehouse doorways along with grunts of workers and the shouts of foremen.

Eventually I came to a tall building made from green glass: the Land's Shield Northern Aerodrome. A muumuu attendant stood by an elevator. It led to the top platform where citizens boarded large passenger ships to other parts of Laergard and—at, least before the current trade embargoes—to the other continents of Illyria as well.

I moved past the attendant and entered the back warehouse area of the aerodrome where ships were built and repaired. I walked across the bay, passing by smooth frigates, schooners, brigantines, and galleons. An assortment of both Rorn and Aeri workers ran the repair factory —an odd pairing as choosing either one as a starter race dinged you with a negative alignment against the other. In the case of Laergardian aircraft, however, the two antagonistic races had a shared project. Unlike the Arethkarian vessels purely influenced by the Rorn with their iron exterior, Laergardian airships were a hybrid blend of Aeri-infused wood powered by Rorn magitech. It meant the Laergardian fleet was less statistically powerful than Arethkar's, but more nimble and quicker.

At the end of the long factory, I found the *Horizon's Dream*, propped up with scaffolding. It was attended to by an assortment of different workers repairing the damage from earlier today. It was one of the perks of flying under the king's banner, I got free repairs; which was one less expense in what was still an insanely expensive enterprise.

Waiting for me underneath the bowsprit was the mustachioed helmsman.

"I'd like my cut of the ship's earnings before I quit."

Damn. I had hoped he'd only been whining on board the ship earlier. Finding someone to replace him would be tough.

"Is there anyway I can convince you otherwise?"

"Nope. Earnings, please."

The last mission had really taken its toll on the crew morale, which was a big problem. Morale was a major part of the game's airship mechanics. I opened up the captain's log in my HUD and poured over the stats of the *Horizon's Dream*.

Horizon's Dream

Type: Air Frigate
Size: Large
Turning Radius: Wide
Classification: Warship
Min. Crew: 16
Crew: 24/200
Cannon(s): 14/32
Cargo: 36/80 (tonnage)

Speed: Fast
Crystal Mana Fuel: 30%

Food Supply: Low
Health: 45% (Good)
Crew Morale: Unhappy
Gold: 10,000

I see. The crew morale had tipped into the negative. I opened up the explanation for how crew morale worked; no matter how many times I read it, it was still a difficult balancing act to keep a crew happy while doing insanely dangerous missions. I reviewed the information in my HUD.

Info: Crew Morale

A sky captain is nothing without his crew. The crew morale is always decreasing based on multiple factors: how long you've been out in the sky, the crew's cut of the earnings, and the general food (and alcohol) supply onboard the ship. The key to morale, then, is to pay your crew as much as possible in gold, meat, and wine. Be greedy and keep everything for yourself and you'll soon be walking the plank into the clouds.

Crew morale status can only ever be in one of five states: overjoyed, happy, content, unhappy, defiant. A positive crew runs the ship faster and increases cannon reload speed, a negative crew will operate at a more sluggish pace.

I clicked on another window in the HUD to open up the ship's earnings.

Earnings (- mandatory expenses)

Arethkarian Supply Vessel = +200,000 gold coins
Extra Loot = +1,200 gold coins

Crystal Mana Fuel = -20,000 gold coins

Accept earnings (and expenses): yes/no?

Awesome. The supplies on board the ship were part of the mission and so didn't count towards our earnings, however, the actual ship and the remaining loot on the fallen soldiers did, giving us a brilliant pay-out. I gladly clicked accept and the *Horizon's Dream* gold stat rushed up to 192,000 gold coins. Fantastic. A new screen popped up afterwards.

Are you ready to divide the earnings and pay out the crew: yes/no?

This was the tricky part. I closed the window, knowing I would return to it in a few minutes.

There were different regulations and systems available on how to divide the ship's earnings. Sky pirate captains were known to keep up to 50% of a ship's earnings for themselves and have the rest of the crew vie for the rest. It was a bit shortsighted, though, as such divisions had a strong likelihood of creating a mutinous crew. Greed clearly played a part in sky pirates having such short life expectancies. The current system we had agreed to was after upkeep the earnings got divided equally amongst the entire crew. We were all risking our lives out there, we all deserved to be recompensed fairly. The difficult part was the crew morale declined every time I purchased anything for the ship, eating away at the individual crew member's profits. The morale would shoot up into the positive zone as soon as I divided the earnings and paid out the crew; however, once I did so, I wouldn't be able to afford any of the expensive and desirable upgrades for the ship. Worse, even with the earnings before pay-out, I wouldn't be able to upgrade it as much I'd like to, due to the crew morale status already at "unhappy." If I spent too much of their cut on the boat, they'd quit. For this very reason, I was thankful we didn't have to pay for repairs.

I opened up a new window titled, *Upgrades.* I was given multiple options:

+*Ship Upgrades*
+*Ship Tools*
+*Hire Crew Members*

I clicked ship upgrades to see if anything new was available. Certain upgrades came in and out of availability depending on the state of the aerodrome you were in; whether it was busy or out of stock of a certain item. A long list of available upgrades to the ship appeared in front of me.

*Additional Cannon (**5,000 gold coins**)*

*Additional Laser Turret (**5,000 gold coins**)*

*Bronze Cannon: Upgrade cannons to a more accurate firing cannon (**15,000 gold coins**)*

Chain Shot: ammunition designed to cripple a ship's masts and sails. Perfect for pillaging rather than sinking ships. (10,000 gold coins)

Copper Plating: Increased maneuverability. Makes it easier to avoid cannon shots and get around enemy ships (25,000 gold coins)

Cotton Sails: Increase ship's speed (10,000 gold coins)

Fine-Grain Powder: Increases range for all cannon types. (15,000 gold coins)

Grape Shot: Hurts crew members more than ship. Good for boarding ships without destroying it (13,000 gold coins)

Iron Scantlings: Reinforce hull of your ship (30,000 gold coins)

Triple Hammocks: Increase your ship's maximum crew capacity. (5,000 gold coins)

Skyfish Trap: Passively catch fish by attaching these to the side of your ship. (3,000 gold coins)

My eyes glowed across the available upgrade list. I was like a kid in a candy shop with a pocketful of birthday money. I only had one or two available purchases before the crew morale dropped to defiant though. If I pissed off my band of sailors to such an extent, I risked the crew walking out on me, taking their final set of earnings with them. I had to make my limited purchases worth it, so with that in mind, I checked to see what specialists were available to join our ship. I clicked back on the window in my HUD and accessed the specialist for hire tab. A long list of specialized crew members appeared with additional tabs to see who specifically was currently looking for a job.

Specialists For Hire (See additional sub tabs for available specialists and pay requirements)

Carpenter: Can repair hull damage

Cook: Slows down the speed by which the crew's morale decreases

Cooper: Reduces the amount of food consumed per crewman, allowing your ship to travel longer with less food

Gunner: The gunner increases your ship's canon reload rate

Navigator: Increases ship speed

Quartermaster: Decreases the number of crew deserters

Sailmaker: Mends sail damage while soaring through the sky. Also helps improves reefing ability and saves on crystal mana fuel

Surgeon: Dedicated lower deck healer. Reduce losses of crew

All of these positions were worth hiring somebody for,

but even still I closed the tab. I was going to hold off on hiring new people until I was sure about whether we were flying to Ariellum; I didn't want to hire anyone on false pretenses.

I opened the other tab and reviewed the available upgrades again. Additional cannons and laser turrets weren't worth it to me, though the chain shot and grapeshot ammunition did strike me as handy given so much of our sky battles involved us boarding enemy ships. I also liked the cotton sails for the increase to our ship's speed and the iron scantlings to boost our defense.

There was also the less practical skyfish traps. They weren't too expensive and they opened a potentially new revenue source for the ship, which was important; not every voyage ended with a giant cash cow prize like a supply vessel. The only other way to make gold outside of skyfishing, stealing enemy airships, and doing missions was *discoveries*. The skyfarer's guild in all the major cities across Illyria offered big payouts to anyone who discovered lost artifacts, locations, and rare items in their travels throughout the treacherous skies. The cloud oceans remained a dangerous and mysterious place and the skyfarer's guild would pay a pretty penny to those who offered any illuminating information on the vast aerial world.

I went with the skyfish trap as my first purchase and given it was the cheapest upgrade, I doubted it would rock the crew morale. I selected the skyfish trap option and clicked purchase. A new screen appeared.

Congratulations on your newest purchase: [Skyfish Trap]!
Please note it will take up to a few hours for your upgrades to appear on your ship

The crew morale remained at unhappy. Good, because they were definitely not going to be pleased after my next purchase. I chose the upgrade *iron scantlings* to increase the defense of the ship. "More work!?" groaned the workers already doing the repair job.

Congratulations on your newest purchase: [Iron Scantlings]! Please note it will take up to a few hours for your upgrades to appear on your ship

I checked the ship's status again and as expected, the crew was pissed.

Warning! Crew morale has fallen to defiant. Any more actions that work to lower morale could cause unruly consequences

Fair enough. I had spent 35,000 gold coins of their profit. I'd be pissed too, especially considering how much of a beating we took today. I opened up the tab I'd closed earlier and reviewed it, clicking, "pay-out crew."

Please confirm earnings division: 157,000 gold coins to be split evenly across 24 crew members, equally 6,541 gold coins per member.

Accept/decline?

I accepted the earnings division and the gold disappeared from the ship's status screen while a big chunk of gold entered my own inventory.

I closed the screen and rubbed my head.

The mustachioed helmsman was still standing in front of the ship. "Thank you for my payment. Please consider this my formal resignation."

He strode off in a huff.

I sighed and rubbed my eyes. Footsteps echoed across the aerodrome. Serena strolled across the ship repair bay towards me.

"Good afternoon captain."

"Don't call me that," I said.

She smirked. "You don't like being captain? I thought you loved being heroic and doing the right thing. I never thanked you for valiantly saving me earlier."

"I know you think I overdid it," I said. "But it's hard to know what's right and wrong in a split-second. I didn't have time to think, only time to *act*."

Serena's nose twitched. "It's fine—the guy was literally about to stab me in the neck with two daggers. I think you had the moral high ground. Or, you know, the less immoral low ground."

I sighed and shook my head. I wanted to change the subject. I started walking out of the aerodrome, passing engineers and newly built ships, shadowing over us in their brilliant fresh glory. "What are we going to do about this quest?"

"Something about it doesn't feel right," said Serena, walking beside me. "I know Theobold and Fergus mean well, but seeking a weapon powerful enough to destroy an entire continent? A weapon so destructive stays buried for a reason."

"But what if unearthing the weapon saves us?" I said, stepping out of the aerodrome and back into the engineering district. "What if it saves Land's Shield? Saves

6

A lot needed to get done before we set sail. We had given ourselves the rest of the day and night to prepare. We needed to restock the ship for fuel and food. We needed to decide on any other upgrades we'd add to the ship. We needed to recruit more crew members, including a new dedicated airship pilot and navigator. We still needed to convince Shade to come along. And...

"You need to level up," said Theobold, stroking his beard amidst his new chambers in the keep's tower. "Tier-one and level 15. You're far too low."

"Don't scold me—you're the one who made this game."

The old wizard shook his head and sighed, "Oh how I wish I'd never been apart of this damned project, but here I am." He shook his head. "I've spent too many years in here wallowing and I won't do anymore of it. At least, not for the rest of the days. Follow me Clay. It's time you got some formal *training*."

The old wizard picked up his staff, lying between two stacks of old worn books, overtop a carpet of scrolls and loose paper full of arcane scribbles and grocery lists. He swung the staff onto his back and looked around. He patted his pants to see if he was forgetting anything.

"It's the great thing about living in a castle Clay," said Theobold. "You don't need to worry about keys and locking the door because you live behind a giant stone wall and pay people to stop any trespassers. It's brilliant."

The Rorn stroked his beard even faster and nodded his head, his eyes bulging with excitement. I was concerned this man was about to give me, in his own words, "formal training."

He led the way down the tower. We were soon walking through the city, enjoying the midday sun. We walked through the noble district with their beautiful gated houses and pretty canals, through the night court and the Grand Casino Palace. We were taking a route I'd taken before, a few weeks ago when solving the mystery of vanishing citizens in Land's Shield. We eventually arrived at the broken docks, the poorest area in all the city. It was an abandoned extension to the aerodrome, where wayward orphans and the perennially homeless slept at night.

Moving south we arrived at the city's walls and approached a door. Theobold swung it open, revealing a damp stone stairwell. I followed behind the wizard as we descended deeper until we reached the bottom and found ourselves in the city's sewers.

It was brighter than it had been on my previous excursion into the city's necropolis. To the left, the cylindrical stone passageway ended, opening wide into the endless sky. A river of green sewage drifted downward at our feet and off the passageway into the cloud ocean. I guess the waste had to go somewhere and a bottomless sky wasn't a bad place to put it.

"Yuck," I said, stepping around the flowing sludge and

onto the narrow walkway further down the sewer. "Why have you brought me here?"

"You'll see soon enough," said Theobold, walking deeper into the damp passageway, away from the light of day and into the darkness.

The stench got worse the further we went. The potent mix of shit, piss, dirt, rubbish and rain water was a pungent assault on the senses. Theobold pulled his staff from behind his back and created a glowing rod. We eventually entered a larger chamber. He conjured a fireball in his hand and whipped it across the room, lighting a torch. He did so four more times, illuminating the whole room.

I preferred it in the dark.

Across the stone chamber were rats the size of watermelons. They had fat hunched backs, sharp teeth, and glowing red eyes. Their thick tails were pink and fleshy. Their fur was wet and full of patches, exposing enflamed skin beneath. There were loads of them, walking back and forth, sniffing the cracks of the stone floor.

They ranged from levels 10 to 13.

"So these will be the mobs, you'll be grinding today," said Theobold. "They have a pretty quick respawn rate from what I remember *and* since you'll be fighting them alone, you'll gain all the experience points for yourself. Partying up is a good long-term survival strategy and can net you huge amounts of experience if you do enough quests together, but for sheer power leveling, you're actually better off solo. Some people would argue with me, but hey, that's how we're going to do it today."

"You're going to make me take on all these rats by myself?"

"I'll be here. Importantly—*not as a party member*—but I'll back you up or heal you if need be."

This was crazy. Theobold was a stronger version of my class, but he knew how little actual defense we had, how squishy the class was. Taking on these rats—especially if I accidentally aggroed more than one of them—would be an absolute death sentence.

"We're going to do focus training today," said Theobold. "I should've taught you this stuff earlier, but I thought you'd get the hang of it, but it appears you're more *apprentice* than mage."

"Screw you man."

"Your trash talk needs improvement too," smiled Theobold. "But never mind that now. Let's call up your stats and ability sheet."

I checked my stats in my HUD.

Clay Hopewell
Level 15
Race: Aeri (Eldra)
Class: Apprentice Mage

HP: 156
MP: 74

ATKP: 3
MTKP: 70
TGH: 5
SPIRIT: 55
LUCK: 3

I was slowly growing more powerful, but not as quickly as I would've liked. Next, I opened up my class skill sheet, looking over the skills and abilities available to me. I'd been hoarding my class skill points; not sure what exactly to do with them. I had seven at the moment. My class skill sheet shined out across my HUD.

Fire (Damage Based): Fireblast (Level 5) > Flame Breath (Level 10) > Volcanic Eruption (Level 15) > Supernova (Level 20)

Fire (Support/Utility Based): Flame Dodge (Level 5) > Flame Wall (Level 10) > Ring of Fire (Level 15) > Summon Phoenix (Level 20)

Water (Damage Based): Water Blast (Level 5) > Ice Wave (Level 10) > Frozen Ground (Level 15) > Conjure Ice Blade (Level 20)

Water (Support/Utility Based): Healing Mist (Level 5) > Status Cure (Level 10) > Tidal Protect (Level 15) > Restorative Storm (Level 20)

Air (Damage Based): Air Blast (Level 5) > Lightning Ball (Level 10) > Relentless Crackle (Level 15) > Plasma Beam (Level 20)

Air (Support/Utility Based): Lightning Cage (Level 5) > Shocking Speed (Level 10) > Electric Blink (Level 15) > Skull Shock (Level 20)

Earth (Damage Based): Earthquake (Level 5) > Sand Storm (Level 10) > Stone Shards (Level 15) > Gravity Tremor (Level 20)

Earth (Support/Utility Based): Ruptured Ground (Level

*5) > Stone Skin (Level 10) > Spike Field (Level 15) >
Summon Rock Golem (Level 20)*

All the spells looked so cool and I didn't want to screw up my build, so I'd been holding off on spending more of my class skill points until I knew better.

"How many class skill points do you have available?" grunted Theobold.

"Seven," I said.

"Okay, listen closely, I want you to add these spells. Are you listening? Okay, here we go. Teach yourself flame wall, frozen ground, air blast, and electric blink."

"But—"

"Do it. These spells are all very important."

I did as he told me and spent the class skill points, gaining the ability to cast four new spells. I took in their descriptions.

Flame Wall (Level 1)
Ability: Create a wall of flame between you and your opponent
MP Cost: 10

Frozen Ground (Level 1)
Ability: Create an area of pure frozen ice
MP Cost: 13

Air Blast (Level 1)
Ability: Push back a foe with a deadly gust of wind
MP Cost: 7

Electric Blink (Level 1)
Ability: Teleport up to six meters away

MP Cost: 20

"You done over there?" asked Theobold. "Before we start our lessons, I want you to attack the rat over there. I wanna see how much you know already."

Theobold walked over to a corner and jumped up to a ledge.

"That rat?" I said, pointing to a fat one in the middle.

"Any rat."

I turned to a rat at the opposite corner to me. It was off on its own and would hopefully not attract the other rats to fight me.

I gulped and then ran to the rat and stretched out my arms, casting lightning cage. A purple burst of lightning whipped out of my palm and encircled the oversized vermin. It squealed in pain as it squirmed in the paralyzing electric cage. Next I gathered both my hands together to create a molten-sized fireball. I unleashed the blast, burning the gray hairs of the creature. The electric bars of the lightning cage faded away and the rat scurried towards me, leaping with its jaws wide open. I triggered flame dodge, sliding across the sewer floor, leaving a trail of flames. The rat was so aggroed, it ran through the flames towards me, stacking up burning debuffs along the way. It died, collapsing on the floor, burnt to a crisp at my feet.

+350 EXP!

I turned towards Theobold and bowed. *Pretty decent.* I killed the creature without it landing any hits.

"What do you think?" I said.

Theobold made a face. "Not great."

My stomach sunk. "What do you mean?"

Theobold shook his head and contemplated for a moment. "You really have a lot to learn." He jumped off his pedestal and walked towards me. "You're treating your spells as individual moves. Wielding magic isn't just summoning different abilities to do stuff for you, but rather conjuring the elements and manipulating them together to create awesome results. There are hidden abilities, combos—one's that won't ever appear in your HUD—but once learned, open whole new possibilities for your class."

I stood dumbfounded. There was always so much more to learn, so much to do. "What combos can you teach me?"

"Well for starters, I don't know why you attacked one individual rat. Your strengths as a mage are both ranged damage and AoE-style attacks. I liked your blunt use of fire blast, but you'd be better served casting earthquake at your enemies and then using fireblast on top of your earthquake spell."

"You mean, attack them while they're being damaged from earthquake?"

"No," said Theobold. "Attack the crumbling earth and you'll create burning ground, adding extra damage and a chance of burning debuff on the entire AoE."

"Sounds hardcore."

"Exactly. Try attacking the rats again."

Theobold returned to the pedestal in the corner, standing watch over the sewer environment.

Four rats lingered in the center of the room. My fingers twitched with giddy excitement. I'd take them all on this time.

I stretched my arms out and pulled at the ground beneath the group of rats. The floor shook and crumbled, stone cracking apart, turning into jagged spears, stabbing the group of rats. They jumped off their feet in panic. I wasted no time, conjuring a fireball in both my hands and whipping them at my AoE spell. The fire blast smashed into the jagged rocks and all the stones in the AoE turned ember hot, smoke emanating off the rocks. Cripple and burning debuffs stacked underneath the rats' health bars. Their eyes flared and they gathered their balance on the stone. They ran towards me.

Shit.

These rats were higher level than the one I first attacked. I'd managed to take out half of each of their HP—so cumulatively two full rat's worth of HP—but, so long as they were alive and coming for me, none of that mattered.

I triggered flame dodge, shooting myself across the chamber's stone platform. It was the perfect opportunity for earthquake but I had another thirty seconds on the recast buffer.

"Here's another combo," yelled Theobold from up above. "Frozen ground plus air blast."

I ran from the gang of rats, kiting them across the chamber in a ridiculous zigzag pattern. I didn't understand Theobold's suggested combo. Was he telling me to freeze the ground and then push them off it? Oh wait. I got it.

I spun around and pushed both my arms out in front of me. My fingertips turned icy cool as I created a big circle of ice right behind the incoming rats. They leapt in the air, claws drawn and teeth barred. A gust of wind blasted forth from my hands. The propulsive air flung the rats through the air, their bodies slamming and skidding into the new plate of ice. Their legs trembled as they attempted to gain balance, lifting their feet with a frosted slowness.

Perfect.

"Now for the combo again," shouted Theobold.

I summoned earthquake, destroying the field of ice, the

jagged stones tearing into the flesh of the weakened rats. Next I conjured a ball of flames in my hand and whipped it at the AoE spell, igniting it with fiery power.

The rats screamed and experience from their deaths came rolling into my HUD.

+455 EXP!
+455 EXP!
+455 EXP!
+455 EXP!

I breathed heavily in and out. Oh man. So much power. So many experience points. I would level super quickly in no time.

I went through the same motions again until I had cleared the chamber of all the rats. Theobold said more would respawn or find their way into the room in a minute or two. While we waited, Theobold told me other counterintuitive ways to use my powers to full effect. *Flame dodge*, for instance, was a defensive move but there was a way to make it offensive. If I kept my back to my target opponent when I triggered flame dodge, I'd launch myself in my enemy's direction. Another cool combo was *healing mist* combined with air blast to create a healing projectile to cure my fellow party members at range. Finally, Theobold showed me how lightning cage was able to cancel incoming attacks if cast at the right second.

So the lessons went, hour upon hour, until the sewer chamber we were in reeked of blood and rat carcasses. I was leveling up by the hour. As the time passed, it had become rote memory: earthquake, fireblast, flame dodge, ice wave, air blast, repeat. I was learning a powerful rotation to handle multiple mobs at once and soak in experience. It was a risky combo for sure though. If Theobold wasn't there to watch over me, I'm not sure I'd have the balls to take on five or six rats at once. If they got anywhere close to me and all landed a hit, I was a dead man.

The stone embers burnt the flesh of the rats to death, their skin melting off their bone and another wave of experience points stacked up in my HUD.

+490 EXP!
+490 EXP!
+490 EXP!
+490 EXP!
+490 EXP!

Congratulations! You have leveled up (Level 20)
You gain +4 HP
You gain +1 MP
You have (3) unused attribute points that can be applied to any of your five base stats.
You have (8) unused class skill points that can be applied to your class skill tree to unlock new moves or level up existing ones.

Holy shit. My arms ached, my head pulsed with pain, every part of my body felt sick and tired. I put the three attribute points into magic attack power as I had been placing most of them into my spirit over the last few levels to increase my pool of MP. My new stats were very satisfying.

Clay Hopewell
Level 20
Race: Aeri (Eldra)

Class: Apprentice Mage

HP: 176
MP: 90

ATKP: 3
MTKP: 74
TGH: 5
SPIRIT: 66
LUCK: 3

I can't believe I'd gotten to level 20. The possibilities from here were endless: Level 20 abilities I was now able to unlock, tier-2 classes to explore, new armor sets available in the Trader's Forum. This was awesome.

"What level 20 abilities should I acquire? Are you going to help me pick my tier-2 class?"

"Slow down," said Theobold, walking up to me. He held out his hand. "Congratulations on getting to level 20. That was my goal. The level 20 abilities are extra powerful and will amp your survivability by quite a bit. Your tier-2 class can wait. When the time comes for you to learn your next class, you won't feel the need to ask permission."

"Okay but what abilities do you think I need to learn?"

"You have enough to learn at least two. I wouldn't spend all your points until you know what next class you'd want to be. You're safe to pick two. I can't guide you with this. You need to decide for yourself."

I opened my class skill sheet in my HUD and reviewed the level 20 abilities available to me. The two available to me were *conjure ice blade* and *skull shock*. I had enough points to unlock the others, but I would have to spend points on the earlier spells in the skill tree first to unlock

them. Even still, I reviewed the level 20 abilities open
to me.

Supernova
Ability: Create a massive meteor in the sky that crashes
down on your opponents
MTKP: 300-700
MP Cost: 50

Summon Phoenix
Ability: Summon a deadly phoenix that will fight on your
behalf. Spell duration: 2 minutes.
MP Cost: 50

Conjure Ice Blade
Ability: Create a blade made of the ice so sharp it can cut
through anything. Spell duration: 2 minutes.
MTKP: 250-450
MP Cost: 50

Restorative Storm
Ability: Create an AoE storm that heals all of your party
members
MP Cost: 50

Plasma Beam
Ability: Shoot a destructive laser blast from the palm of
your hands
ATKP: 400-600
MP Cost: 50

Skull Shock

Ability: A fully paralyzing stun ability on any monster.
Duration: 15 seconds
MP Cost: 50

Gravity Tremor
Ability: An AoE earthquake with a horizontal and vertical radius
MP Cost: 50

Summon Rock Golem
Ability: Summon a powerful rock golem that will fight on your behalf. Spell duration: 2 minutes.
MP Cost: 50

These spells were all wicked. They would also cost more than half of my available MP, meaning I'd have to save them for special occasions. I'm sure they had a long re-cast time too. The choices I ultimately settled on were not the choices I would've made a few days ago. Earlier in the week I would've gone for the flashiest moves in the arsenal: supernova and summon phoenix—maybe rock golem to change things up from the fire spells. Yet, after today's training session with Theobold, I was starting to realize how important complimentary abilities were. So in the end, I spent two class skill points, learning *conjure ice blade* and *skull shock*. The choice conserved the most amount of class skill points I had for later and also meant I was in a position to unlock the mage tier-2 class quest.

But I'd save the trial for another day.

"All done?" asked Theobold.

"I think so," I said. "But I have a few questions."

"A few questions! How about, '*Thank you kind Theobold.*'

I just helped you gain five levels and increase your DPS and general fighting ability. What more can I offer you?"

"Well I was wondering some logistics. Why aren't there more players coming down here and power leveling like this?"

Theobold nodded his head and brought his hand to his chin. "Good question. One I've asked myself. Honestly—I think it's the difference between Arcane Kingdom Online being a game and it being one's life." He paused. "As you've told me, the world outside is no more. A.K.O. is people's lives then. It's also hyper realistic and immersive. Look around you, we're in a dark sewer surrounded by bloody rat corpses. This is *disgusting*. Most people aren't going to venture down on their own and do this."

"Shit—are we total sociopaths then?"

Theobold laughed. "No. There's features of the game like pain and violence the engine purposefully dulls one senses to. If we had it any other way, people would suffer too greatly from PTSD inside of here. Early testing showed that to us. We're not down here right now because we're insane —though I do have an ongoing bet with Archades concerning *your* sanity—but because we have a mission to accomplish, a home to protect. In an older game, someone would happily come into a sewer and grind kill a bunch of rats, but in this world—where you can become a master chef, a craftsman, an explorer—why bother with grinding and leveling up? Unless, of course, you're doing it for a real worthwhile purpose."

Damn, Theobold was coming at me with inspirational stuff. It raised another question though.

"You keep saying *we*. Why aren't you coming with us to Ariellum? Why aren't you out there on the battlefield? I remember back in Arondale seeing your stats. You were level 99!"

Theobold sighed and rubbed my shoulder.

"I didn't earn those levels, Clay. I used the Prophetic Seal to make myself more powerful. When I found out I was trapped in this game, I used the special mark to level up faster than normal. The artificial leveling screwed up my build and weakened my stats. I'm level 99 in pretty much name only. My power level is nowhere near there. I have many powerful skills unlocked, but they are considered weaker than the "level one" version of the spell. My level 99 status is a curse I bear for manipulating the game for my own benefits. At the time I told myself I was doing it to help the others trapped inside here, but now I'm not so sure. Heed my warning Clay." The Rorn wizard looked me straight in the eye. "*Many terrible deeds done in times of crisis are rationalized with good intentions, but that does not make them right.*"

7

After leaving the sewers with Theobold, the next thing I had to do was find Shade. He had left the throne room pretty pissed off with the whole idea of seeking out Ariellum and I didn't blame him. The fallen city was mythical to Lirana, their lost mecca. It was blasphemous after its destruction to go seek it out, and yet we needed him on this quest. He was our thief, our rogue, our melee DPS, the man who broke down all the hidden traps on all our quests, and, last but not least, he was the ship's resident drunk and if that wasn't important to morale I didn't know what was.

I started with his favorite pub, The Crooked Bell. I found an empty hole in the wall with one Haeren barmaid polishing glasses while one patron fell asleep at his stool, pint in hand. I went to the Pauper's Pump Room next. No dice. The same thing happened with the Raven's Room, the Artful Alehouse, and the Knight's Brewery.

Where the heck was Shade?

I had one last idea.

As I strolled up to the Haeren Church of the Nine's Orphanage, I found a group of children huddled in a small circle. I heard a voice coming from beyond the children, speaking at their feet.

"You see it's all about misdirection. Have the mark's attention focused elsewhere as you slip your fingers into his pocket, or her purse, or their luggage, or you know—if you're really talented—straight out of his or her hands. What I'm trying to say kids is this: *I believe in you.*"

What was I overhearing?

A cute little Rorn boy, raised his hand. "What if they catch you with your hand in their pocket?"

"*Sorry mister my hand slipped.*"

"What if they don't believe that?"

"*A devilish pixy jumped into your pocket and I wanted to stop it.*"

"Or that?"

"*Over there!*" Shade pointed to me and all the kids turned. He then clapped his hands, "And in a snap of fingers you're gone. See, misdirection again. Alright, now scram. Don't tell the nuns what I taught you."

The kids ran off, leaving Shade and me in the street.

"I was looking everywhere for you," I said. "I practically searched every pub in the city."

"I'm a changed man, Clay. You see—"

"Were you literally not just teaching a bunch of little kids how to steal?

"—look, if you insist, fine, you can buy me one—*no*, two pints—of ale. I know just the place."

Shade and I strolled away from the orphanage and wound our way down the streets until we were standing in front of a brick building, sandwiched between two other buildings. There was a lone black door without any advertisements on it. He opened the door and we stepped into a quiet pub.

Ah, this was a proper Shade establishment. He drank everywhere but this was like the first inn he'd ever taken me to back in Arondale. A thief's pub. It smelled of cheese, wine, and sausage rolls. A crackling fire glowed from a hearth in the center of the room, while quiet cloaked individuals sat at wooden tables alone, drinking from their pitchers of ale. A group of Lirana were playing cards in one corner.

Shade sat down at one of the bar stools and I did the same.

The portly Haeren man poured himself a glass of whisky and asked, "How can I help you?"

"Two ales please," I said.

Shade coughed.

"One for me, one for you, no?"

Shade made a disparaging face.

Oh, right. "Sorry—make that three ales."

The bartender smirked, took a sip of his whisky glass and got to work. He bent down and pulled three pint glasses from a cupboard and one by one pulled a metal lever and let amber liquid pour into the glass. My eyes glazed over with delight and soon enough, the glorious pint with the top rim of foam was sitting in front of me. I jealously looked over at Shade who had gone for two pints. He may have been skinny but he had an amazing constitution.

Shade took a long sip of his first pint, draining half of it in a single gulp. He swallowed, slouched his shoulders and let out a relaxed sigh. He stared across the bar into the glittering reflections of the bottles lining the wall.

"I'm assuming you saw I accepted the king's quest in the party logs," I said.

"Yep."

"You were pretty adamant about not doing the quest back in the throne room. Do you still feel that way?"

He sniffed and blinked. He still wasn't facing me. "It's this quest. I have my doubts about it. All my life I've thought about Ariellum, thought about what it would be like to grow up there, or even visit. The Lirana have made their peace with their alliance with the Haeren and other races, accepted their lot as merchants and nomads, confided to certain quarters of certain cities, adopting Haeren celebrations as their own. It isn't all bad, but it isn't what we truly want, there's a hole in our hearts. Part of me thinks it's punitive. The hole, the feeling of something missing. It's my people's punishment for creating the Ultriga Weapon in the first place."

I took a sip of my pint. "I guess it comes down to: what are you willing to do to protect those you love?"

Shade went quiet. I imagined he was thinking about the kids at the orphanage who looked up to him, Kari, and the rest of us. While the Lirana ruminated, I considered all those I'd lost on Earth to the deadly ZERO virus. My parents, my brother, everyone I'd ever known. I'd done nothing to help them, especially my brother, who had done everything in his power to help me survive, to have my mind uploaded into this game. He pulled strings with the government, fought angry rioters ready to kill and take us for all we were worth, laid his life on the line to get me where I am. What had I done for him? Nothing. In the years preceding the outbreak of the virus, I had moved away from home and barely kept in touch. I'd send a postcard once a year, if anything at all.

I did nothing to help my brother, but I could still make it up to him. I could help others like he had helped me.

Shade turned to me and smiled. "Nothing I do or say is going to stop you, huh?"

"I don't care how high your Luck stats are, I'm going on this mission."

Shade stretched his arms. "You really are a crazy bastard, you know? I guess I'm crazy too as I gotta come with you. Let's agree now the ship has to have a well-stocked kitchen and we better have quality liquor too. And cheese. And fruit. And did I say liquor? That's the most important thing we need on this quest."

"Agreed! Do you know what else we need? A sky navigator; and Shade, my friend, I know just where to find one."

8

Below the Grand Casino Palace in the Night Court of Land's Shield existed a gladiatorial arena, an illegal underground fighting ring for those to gamble and satiate their bloodlust. Shade and I, through a snafu I 100% blame on my Lirana thief pal, had previously been contestants. I was in disbelief I had returned here willingly.

Bright lights glowed in the center of the pit as a fighter ran head to head with the largest wolf I'd ever seen. It was thick and beastly and shadowed over the Rorn brawler going up against it. Its yellow eyes glinted outward. Its snout scrunched into a growl. The wolf barred its teeth and dug its claws into the sand of the pit.

The audience cheered at the wolf's display of anger and rage. It was the crowd favorite.

The Rorn fighter was a stout muscular man with a thick gray beard falling below his hardened pecks. He wore an orange headband to keep his hair from falling in his eyes. A single beaded braid fell down beside his left temple. His thick arms were weapons of muscle and strength. Bronze bracers wrapped around his wrists. He wore baggy cloth pants offering quick movement speed and dexterity. He was a brawler, A.K.O.'s equivalent of the Monk or Pugilist class.

"Hey, don't we know him?" said Shade, as we walked down the staircase between seating areas.

We did. He'd given us advice when we'd been imprisoned in this very arena. He was currently wearing slave's bracers. The bronze arm bands would keep him enslaved until he earned his freedom in these fighting pits.

"Don't tell me, you're thinking *he's* going to be our next navigator? He's a brute!"

"Has no one ever told you not to judge a book by its cover?"

"I have," said the Lirana. "But I've come to believe that is false advice, peddled by charlatans. I *always* judge a book by its cover; even well-hidden truths have a way of making themselves known on the prettiest of surfaces."

"Whatever you say man," I said. "The guy mentioned while we were imprisoned—because of you by the way—that he knew how to operate an airship. We need a player—not a hired stranger—with insider knowledge on how airships work."

We hurried down the arena's steps to get a closer view of the fight. I was prepared to strike a deal, buy him outright, or break him out of here myself. If we were going to stop Arethkar from enslaving its Chosen, we needed to start with the people in chains on our own continent.

We moved further down the steps, passing a goblin selling candied apples. A group of rat creatures—Skren, they were called—handed the goblin some coins and walked away, licking their apples as they took a spot on the stone benches of the stadium.

In the pit, the wolf roared. It dug its claws into the ground and pulled its neck back like a slingshot readying to shoot itself forward. Its legs and claws strained as it pulled its body towards its target, launching into the air.

The stretched-out claws came for the fighter's flesh first, but the Rorn slid back and jumped out of the way. The over-sized wolf widened its mouth and pushed its neck forward ready to take a chomp. The fighter retaliated by clenching his fists and stretching his arms out at the side. A swirl of blue light enveloped his body. He let out a bellowing roar of his own, creating a tremor as far as the stalls. The gray wolf's fur prickled from the attack, sliding backwards from the tremor, taking 4% of its HP off.

The wolf shook its head. It was startled, unused to such retaliation. The battle wasn't going to be as quick and easy as it was used to. The large beast let out a massive roar. Spit flew from its mouth as a gust of wind pushed the brawler back a step.

The fighter's face remained calm in front of the fearful opposition. He clenched his fist and crossed his arms, knocking his wrists against each other. A swirl of wind spun around his person from his feet to his head. *A speed buff.*

The brawler ran across the pit, straight for the monstrous wolf. Red energy swirled around his right hand as he screamed with rage. He threw the empowered fist right into the creature's snout. The wolf let out a whelp and the audience gasped. The wolf stumbled back. Blood dripped from its gums. It quickly retaliated by whipping its tail in the direction of the fighter. The Rorn leaned into it, holding up his arms like a boxer blocking a punch. His skin crusted and flaked with a layer of stone and met the attack head on. The two moves nullified each other.

The brawler jumped in the air, purple arcane tendrils of smoke flowing out of his fist. He delivered an uppercut punch below the wolf's jaw. The attack sent the wolf into the air. The brawler jumped after it. The fighter clutched onto the wolf's fur and arched back his arm for another punch. When the fist landed right in the center of the wolf's head, a beam of energy followed it right across the wolf's body. Two entities fell back to the ground together, making a massive thud and cloud of smoke.

The debris cleared and the wolf's body laid across the arena floor split in half, organs and entrails leaking out of either side of it. The brawler stood between the two halves of the wolf's corpse, breathing heavily.

The audience roared and bellowed around us. A fight broke out in the stands on the opposite end of the arena. Two Muumuu had made a private bet of their own and one party was very upset with the outcome.

Goblins rushed across the arena to clean up the mess of the dead monster wolf. An announcer appeared at the front of the ring above the stands. He held a glowing crystal device in front of his mouth, allowing him to project his voice.

"Wowee! Everybody give a big round of applause for Jackson Thorne everybody. Now tonight's celebrations are almost over. Tonight is Jackson's final night with us. Will he leave us in death or freedom? Can he survive the next and last fight of this evening? A battle with the Mother Herax!"

Loud thumping footsteps came from down a tunnel locked behind a caged portcullis. What horrible creature was being drawn from the casino's menagerie of monstrosities?

An Orc whispered to a Lirana bandit in the stands in front of us, "Is it even safe for them to bring that thing out here?"

The portcullis cage was raised and emerging from the dark shadows was the Mother Herax: a dinosaur-dragon hybrid. It took the shape of a tyrannosaurus rex with large powerful back legs and a smaller set of clawed hands in its upper body. Its body was coal black and its abdomen glowed with orange ember beneath its scaly skin, exposing the sinewy web connecting all the tissue. Smoke leaked from its nostrils and out the side of its neck. Its jaw was four feet long, meaning when it opened its mouth fully, exposing its giant sharp teeth and long lizard-like tongue, it had a massive target radius; not to mention such jaws would be able to rip bodies and bones apart with ease.

If Jackson was going to be our future sky pilot, odds were he wasn't going to get free from his servitude tonight. Not with him facing a fire-breathing tyrannosaurus-rex on his own.

The Herax stretched out its neck, eyeing the entire audience. Its mere breaths made the floor at our feet tremble. The owners of the arena saw her as a monster to fight other contestants, but the Herax itself wasn't so specific; it would eat all of us.

A man wearing a fur vest cupped his hands around his mouth and projected his voice, hollering at the Mother Herax. He chanted and the dinosaur nodded. It focused its eyes on Jackson Thorne below her in the pit. The chanting man must have been a druid or tamer class.

A group of black-robed mages headed down the aisle on the other side of the arena pit. They cast spells one by one, shooting blue and golden orbs of support magic onto the Mother Herax. Status buffs lined up under its HP bar, giving it better critical hit rate, stronger attacks, higher defense, and on it went.

"What the hell?" I said. "Is nobody going to call interference?"

The goblin in front of us looked up at me and shrugged.

9

Our departure from the Grand Casino Palace was more than a little awkward. Jackson had no belongings to gather and the Rorn guards who worked for the arena offered us stony looks as the three of us exited the casino into the back alley.

The sky was in the fleeting moments of twilight. Our day of planning was over. We needed to return to the keep and look over the remaining preparations.

Newly freed, Jackson was understandably skeptical of our offer to join us on the *Horizon's Dream*. He was grateful for our help in the fight back there, though, so he agreed to come with us to the keep and let us try and convince him more. Plus we were offering free food and board for the night whether he chose to set sail with us in the morning or not.

We walked through the streets, mostly in silence. It was hard to know what to talk about with Jackson. Small talk wasn't appropriate. It took a moment for Shade to catch onto this.

"Tell me Jackson: are you more of a lager man or an ale guy? Or don't tell me: secret wine connoisseur?"

"Whatever gets me drunk," grunted Jackson.

"I've never heard wiser words," said Shade, looking to me like a spouse impressed with someone else's partner.

"Now tell me Jackson: what have you been dying to do since you were locked up?"

The man didn't answer Shade. He simply looked around at the bustling streets. The shop owners closing up their businesses, players heading towards inns after a day of adventuring, and air trams flying by overhead. He was watching life unconstrained by the enslaved debuff. The sight of it all kept him silent.

Shade scratched the back of his head and kept quiet himself.

Back at the keep, we found Serena and Kari in the bailey practicing their abilities. Serena was thrusting her blade over and over while Kari conjured her healing abilities again and again. Repeated use of skills helped them level up.

Kari and Serena had bonded over the last few weeks. They both played crucial roles in our fighting formation: tank and healer. Their whole relationship had to be built on trust and faith in one another. Serena would take all the hits so long as Kari promised to keep her alive. A strong bond of friendship was forming between the two of them; though sometimes I worried when I walked by and the two of them giggled, like they'd been gossiping about me. I smiled and let them have their fun. I had much more significant things to worry about. We all did.

"Well where have you been?" said Serena, sheathing her sword on her back and placing her hands on her hips.

"Getting Shade back on board the quest train," I said.

"I'm still not on board, but I don't want you all to die

without me there to help you," said Shade, crossing his arms.

"Who's this?" said Kari, walking up to us, looking up at Jackson wide-eyed.

"Our new navigator," I said, beaming a smile at Jackson. I quickly added, "*Maybe.*"

"Well, now is as good a time as any to explain how you acquired an airship and why you need me specifically to fly it?"

I was about to launch into a whole summary of my time in A.K.O. when the sound of smashed glass echoed across the courtyard.

"INTRUDERS!" yelled a guard.

An alarm bell rang across the courtyard. Armed soldiers fled out of their barracks and along the walls.

"What's happening?" said Kari.

"Everyone follow me," I said, running up the steps towards the keep, heading in the direction of the shattered glass. *The king. Theobold. Tell me they were okay.*

We entered the darkened throne room, shattered glass laid across the floor. A thick strand of moonlight came through the destroyed glass window.

We walked into the hall, weapons ready for an ambush. I stepped towards the glass and found a stone brick on the ground. What the?

A scream came from up above. Theobold's Tower.

I hurried to the end of the hall and entered the tower staircase towards Theobold's lodgings. I ran up the steps, bashing my way into the room.

Papers were strewn everywhere, while blood leaked across the floor.

"Theobold!" I yelled, finding the old Rorn wizard at less than 10% HP on the floor of the room. I materialized an HP potion and poured it into his mouth. "Kari attend to his wounds. Can you speak Theobold? What happened? Are the intruders still here? What did they want?"

Theobold lifted his shaking hand, pointing above us. "Watch...out..."

A brown metallic ball flew through the air and landed between us. Purple smoke leaked from it. The billowing clouds of purple made it hard to see through the room. Everyone's coughs added to the hysteria. A shuffling noise echoed through the room. Another window shattered. *The intruders were still here.*

I conjured an energy ball in my hand, cutting a light through the smoke. "Shade—are you sensing the intruders?"

"This way—follow me."

Shade led the way to the window. Two shadows rushed across the western walls of the keep. We jumped out, landing onto the stone wall and shattered glass. One shadow ran off into the distance, while another spun around. The intruder was cloaked in all black, like a ninja assassin, but the way he moved his hands to cast a spell suggested he wasn't the ninja class. Blue smoke oozed from his fingertips as he conjured a large bear-like creature. The ferocious animal ran at us, its stats appearing in my HUD.

Spirit Bear
Level 14
HP: 670
MP: 17

Silver knives glistened through the air, zooming by overtop the incoming beast. One swooshed past my head, barely missing me while another hit Shade right in the shoulder, flinging him back.

"Shade!"

I stretched both my arms out and forcefully pushed the air in front of me, triggering air blast, and pushing the spirit bear back.

The intruder turned around and headed off with his partner, leaving us to deal with their distractions. Shit. They were getting away.

"Clay," said Shade, ripping the knife from his shoulder, gasping. "Leave the bear to me. Go after the enemy."

The intruders were now shadows in the night, sprinting across the keep's walls. They were escaping while their spirit bear kept us distracted. I let off another air blast and knocked the bear back. I then created a long stretch of ice between the bear and us.

"I won't leave until back-up comes."

The bear galloped across my plate of ice, slipping and falling in its eagerness to come attack and devour us.

"Clay go! They're getting away," yelled Shade, blood gushing now out of his shoulder.

I grabbed him and hugged him and let the healing mist surround us both. His HP shot back up, the wound in his shoulder stitched itself back together.

The bear got across my field of ice and was pissed off. Lifting up one of its blue translucent spirit claws, swiping down at Shade and me. I flamed dodged backwards, leaving a trail of fire across the stone wall of the keep. Shade jumped to the side.

I conjured a ball of flames in my hand and whipped it at the spirit bear's chest. Its HP was below 50%.

"Back-up is here," said Serena, jumping from the broken

glass window of Theobold's tower, slashing her sword into the spirit bear.

"Go!" Shade shouted.

I electric blinked past the spirit bear onto the other side of the wall and sprinted in the direction of the intruders. They had scaled the walls and gone through the city. I was on the ground level, looking past the evening street and pedestrians for the two black-cloaked figures. Where had they gone? They had too much of a head start on me.

I cast shocking speed and sprinted down the street, looking every which way. I ran past a side street and saw two figures dashing in the distance.

There we go.

I electric blinked down the alley three more times, closing the distance between us. I materialized an MP potion and took a swig.

"Stop!" I yelled.

I hurried after them. My heart beating. My throat burning.

I turned a corner. I was now at the broken docks in southwestern Land's Shield. Between the shanty towns and dilapidated remains of the old aerodrome expansion, were the two cloaked individuals, revving the engine for a small air boat.

I picked up the pace, dashing towards them.

The pink exhaust of the mana engine glowed and shot them off into the night sky.

They were getting away.

I took a swig of my last MP potion and sprinted across the decrepit docks. I power jumped into the air, creating a pool of mana beneath my feet. I did the math in my head as I jumped across the sky, chasing after the get-away boat. Power jump cost 7 MP and I had a total pool of 90 MP. I had twelve jumps to capture the boat. Six if I wanted to make it back to the broken docks.

With my fourth jump, I was closing the gap between me and the intruders. The broken docks were no longer below my feet. I was now jumping across open cloud ocean. A giant pit formed in my stomach. The night sky spun in dizzy delirium. *Keep going. You can catch up to these guys.*

I put all my strength into my fifth leap. I was going to catch up to them with the sixth. One of the cloaked individuals pulled out a mana pistol and pulled the trigger. A bullet smashed right into my stomach, knocking me backwards in the air. I was scrambling. I'd lost balance and focus on my mana puddles. I was falling deeper into the endless cloud ocean.

The wind knocked the hood back of the intruder who had shot me. The man laughed and I recognized him instantly. Bald head, thick neck with pulsing orange veins.

Oren Kaige.

His distant laugh echoed as I fell further through the sky. I focused on my feet and created a mana puddle. I didn't even jump, standing in the middle of the sky, watching Kaige and his summoner accomplice get away. The faint silhouette of a larger Arethkarian vessel hovered in the far distance, waiting to pick them up.

There was no way I'd catch them now. I didn't have the MP to jump so far into the sky.

The broken docks were above me. I electric blinked once then twice and caught hold of a hanging strip of wood. I climbed onto the dock. My heart pounded. I was out of breath. I'd almost killed myself going after Kaige and his man.

Eyes looked out from the makeshift homes of the broken

docks. They furtively glanced at me with both awe and concern.

I stood up and left. On my way to the keep, I kept thinking about how I was going to explain to the team I'd let the intruders get away.

The team was waiting for me in the throne room. The king was there sitting on his throne and so were his advisors on either side of him. Theobold rested on a nearby chair, his wounds tended to. Shade, Serena, and Kari all stood to one side, arms crossed and contemplative. Jackson Thorne leaned against a pillar, unsure where he fit in amongst all of this.

"They got away," I said. "I'm sorry. I let you all down."

Everyone nodded their heads solemnly.

"It would've been great to know why they had broken in and what Arethkar's plans are," I said. "But seeing no one's gotten hurt—I guess, it's not the end of the world, is it?"

Theobold's face was pale.

"End of the world would be the exact words I'd use right now," said Theobold. "Arethkar is searching for the Ultriga Weapon as well. Worse, those two intruders stole the only map in existence on how to get to it."

10

Arethkar now had a copy of the map to Ariellum. The one trump card we had—our single strongest advantage—was now lost. I had been scrambling to gather a crew of people, I hadn't even stopped to think whether Arethkar might've been spying on us, might have had designs of their own. Things weren't all bad though: Theobold had a facsimile copy of the map, so it wasn't like we'd lost our own directions on how to get there. However, it did mean, we were now racing against the clock to beat General Oren Kaige from unlocking the power of the Ultriga Weapon before us.

Jackson Thorne looked up from the map in the captain's quarters of the *Horizon's Dream*. "It's at least a three days journey from here to the destination on the map. If Arethkar already has a copy we don't have a minute to waste here. We need to set sail at once."

"So you're coming with us?"

The Rorn brawler crossed his arms. "I was hoping to have a more peaceful reintroduction into mainstream society, I'll give you that, but you and Shade saved my butt in the arena. Also, how can I say no to being captain of an airship."

"Well, uh, no. *I'm captain*."

The brawler smirked. "I'm joshing you. I don't want the responsibility of captain. The engine and propellers and sky is all I need."

Shade raised his hand. "Let's say you were captain though. Who would be your first mate?"

He shrugged. "If you wanted the job, I'd give it to you."

Shade raised his finger in the air and yelled, "Hallelujah!"

Kari's cheeks blushed as Shade bellowed the phrase.

"At least, it's better than *bros before hoes*," I said.

"Not to nag," shouted Serena from out on the deck, carrying boxes. "But we still have a lot of work to do."

We all separated to our different tasks. Shade worked on getting the rest of the wine and food stocks on board. Kari checked the cannons were clean and gave tours to all the new basic crew members we had on board. I took a quick look at the ship's stats.

Horizon's Dream

Type: Air Frigate
Size: Large
Turning Radius: Wide
Classification: Warship
Min. Crew: 16
Crew: 33/200
Cannon(s): 14/32
Cargo: 45/80 (tonnage)
Speed: Fast
Crystal Mana Fuel: 200%

Food Supply: High

Health: 100% (Good)
Crew Morale: Overjoyed
Gold: 10,000

These were all good stats. The best possible before a long journey. It would be crucial to maintain them throughout the whole mission; or, at the very least, keep them from diminishing too much, especially the crew morale status. They were still overjoyed from the last payout and the prospects of more pay from the new job. The feelings of bitter resentment towards their captain would come later for sure.

"Oi Captain," called one of the crew member's untying rope and unfurling a sail. "You got a visitor."

Theobold approached the ship.

"What are you doing down here?"

"I came to see you off," said the old Rorn mage. "And I brought you a present."

I met the man on the ground level of the Aerodrome. "Let's see that present then."

Theobold lifted his arms and materializing in his hands from his inventory was pile of clothes and boots.

"A whole new set of gear?"

"I figured you needed an upgrade," said Theobold. "I know you can afford to get your own but you've been so run off your feet you haven't had the time."

I scanned the items and equipped them straight away. I stared in awe at the glorious stats. Everything except my staff was new.

Sky Mage Cloak (DEF: 35 +15 MTKP +10 MP +0.05% MP REGEN Rate. Durability: 8/10)

Sky Mage Pants (DEF: 20 +5 MTKP +5 MP Durability: 9/10)

Sky Mage Gloves (DEF: 8 +5 MP)

Sky Mage Boots (DEF: 10 +Bonus Traction on the decks of airships Durability: 7/10)

Fire Staff (ATKP: 25-40, MTKP: 55-97. +Fire Ruby Upgrade (+30 MTKP, +30 Bonus Fire Damage, +15% Chance to Inflict Burn) REQ: Apprentice Mage Class, Level 10)

The cloak was leaner and more austere than my previous one: stitched together with brown cloth and metal shoulder pads. The gear was fantastic, especially the extra buff. Combined together I had an extra 20 MP, meaning I was able to cast one more electric blink if I was caught in a tough jam. The boots' bonus traction onboard the decks of airships would be crazy helpful; keeping balance was a real concern during sky battles.

"Theobold," I said. "This is incredible. Thank you so much."

"You're going to need all the help you can get on this quest. Thank me when you come back alive with the Ultriga Weapon." He sighed and rubbed his hands together. "This evening I worry for the future of A.K.O. more than I ever have in the past."

A bell rang from aboard the ship. Serena came to the balustrade. "Captain Clay Hopewell, this is first mate Serena reporting for duty. We're all packed up and ready to depart sir. Now get your butt up here!"

I smiled at Theobold. "That's my cue."

"Stay safe and good luck."

I nodded my head and hurried back onto the ship. Once on board, the gangplanks were raised, the top men—the crew who worked the sails, climbed up the rope ladders and positioned themselves on the different yards of the sails. We signaled the aerodrome operators for departure. A hole opened in the ceiling of the docking bay and a platform beneath the ship raised us up until we were at the summit of the air station, caught between the glorious city behind us and the expansive cloud ocean in front. The wind blew across my hair and a nervous pit formed in my stomach.

"I'm readying the mana engine now, sir," said Jackson. "If we want to beat the Arethkarian ships to Ariellum, we're going to have to plot a faster route. I propose rather than sailing along the Laergardian coast until we get close to our first port, La-Archanum, we head directly there from here."

"Why weren't we doing that in the first place?"

"The route is more dangerous. We have a high likelihood of interacting with sky creatures. What do you think?"

"We need to claw back any advantage we can," I said. "Let's do it."

Jackson nodded his head and went over to the mana engine on the quarter deck and pulled a lever. A powerful thrust of mana unleashed from the back of the ship, launching us straight into the endless sky.

11

I paced back and forth across my captain's quarters. Serena kept me company, standing by the mullioned windows looking out to the dreamy purple night sky of the cloud ocean. We'd been travelling for a couple of hours now. Half the crew had gone to bed below decks, sleeping in hammocks hung between the beams. The other half performed first watch, along with Jackson, staying on deck and keeping an eye out for any enemy ships or deadly sky monsters.

I turned to Serena. "You haven't spoken in over an hour. What's on your mind?"

She continued looking out into the expansive sea of clouds and stars. "I'm just thinking about the quest. I wasn't sure about it before, but it's become more complicated since then. Arethkar has pushed us into making the decision: we have to get to the Ultriga Weapon before them."

"And what do we do once we get our hands on it?"

"I don't know Clay—I honestly don't."

I fell into the chair at my desk and sighed.

"You know," said Serena. "We've never discussed what

happened before we entered this game. How we ended up here. How we got the ZERO virus." She turned to me, her face solemn and pale. "From the way you've spoken, I've gathered you were the first in your family to contract the virus. I was the opposite. All my family died from it in the early stages. Before the mutations, before people had even given the virus a name or knew what was happening. My dad and I were the last to contract it. We only had enough money for one space in a containment pod to enter A.K.O. My dad wanted me to take it. He only asked I do him one favor. He asked me to end his misery. By that time, he was contained to his bedroom, drenched in sweat, red with fever. The virus was eating him from the inside out. He wanted the pain to end."

Serena's face was pale and she looked like she was going to vomit. Her whole body was shivering. "*What do you do in that scenario? What's right and wrong in a world where the only choices are bad?*"

"What did you do?" I gulped. I wasn't even sure I wanted to know the answer, but I think Serena wanted to tell me. Tell anyone this horrible truth she had kept.

"I took half a tub of painkillers, grinded them with a knife, and then mixed it into his apple juice. I left the room after I'd brought him his drink and called a taxi. I took it to the hospital and started the cognitive upload procedure. I listened to his final request and yet it tears me up inside."

She wiped her eyes. "I still don't know if I did the right thing. He was in pain and no one deserves to suffer in such a way, but what if I'd ignored him? What if I'd let him become a flesh-eater?"

"Then you would've let your dad mutate into a monster," I said. "You didn't have any good options."

"What if there's survivors out there still? What if they

discover a cure? A flesh-eater might be curable. There's no bringing a dead man back to life."

I got up off my chair and approached Serena, grabbing hold of her and holding her tight as she shivered. My own family flashed before my eyes. My brother. My mom. My dad. They were all open possibilities. Dead. Alive. A flesh-eater. A survivor. I didn't know. The uncertainty was tormenting, though it also gave me hope. Serena, whose tears dampened my shoulder, had nothing. Her reality had been lost before she ever escaped into this one. Her blonde hair scratched against my cheek. Her hair—she had changed the color when she had entered the game. She had changed so much of herself and it had so little to do with cosmetics.

"You did what you had to do," I whispered in her ear. "No one would blame you. No one would act differently."

"There must've been another way," she said. "Why didn't I ignore him? Why didn't I leave the house and go to the hospital? Doing something wrong for good reasons doesn't make it right."

I gently rubbed her back and let her cry into my shoulder. Her body heaved as she breathed in and out.

"There's no world for me out there anymore," she cried. "You and others still hope to see your loved ones. I *know* I'm never going to see any of them again. This is my world now Clay. This is my home. Nowhere else."

"Hey now," I said. "It's *our* home and we'll do everything we can to protect it."

Serena was about to say more when there was a knock at the door.

"Who is it?" I yelled. "Can I have five minutes please?"

"Sorry Captain," spoke one of the crewman. "There's an emergency out on deck. Needs urgent attention."

Serena pulled away and wiped her eyes. "It's okay," she said. "Go."

I stood up from my desk and headed to the door of my chambers. I swung it open and stepped out onto the deck. We were deep in a nest of clouds and in every direction were signs of thunder and lightning.

"Jackson," I said, heading up to the quarterdeck to meet him. "What are we looking at?"

The Rorn crossed his thick muscular arms and replied to the roar of thunder with his own dismissive grunt. "There's lightning patches in every direction. I say we stick to our main course and ride it out. We don't really have any other options, unless you want to turn back."

"Do you think that's necessary?"

"Not yet," said the helmsman. "But I'll let you know when I do. Prepare for a bumpy ride."

The navigator headed over to the mana generator and cranked the engine. He was sending us straight into the lightning storm. The Rorn brawler next ordered a group of men to place special generators at the back of the ship.

What was he doing?

The rain slashed against the deck. Thunder roared. My heart beat with terror. Was our journey going to end right as we had begun?

The purple clouds lit up with the bright light of thunder. A tremulous roar echoed all around us, vibrating the wooden floor of the deck.

Shade stepped out from the lower decks, scratching his head. "I had the weirdest dream. I was confronting every person I'd ever swindled at cards all at once. *Not a pretty*—"

A giant roar echoed all around him.

"Oh," he said.

The crackling clouds of lightning were only getting more intense as we got closer to them.

"Jackson—do you know what you're doing?"

The man laughed manically at the clouds. "Questioning your sky pilot, eh? If you were looking for someone sane, maybe a gladiatorial arena wasn't the best place to hire someone from?"

His hair and beard were soaked from the rain.

I winced. A smattering of lightning smashed into the generators. The ship thrust itself further into the sky at a propulsive rate. I slid and fell, knocking head first onto the deck. I closed my eyes and waited for the lightning to strike again and rip our ship in half.

I lay there, the rain no longer knocking against my back. The air grew warmer and clear. I got up from off the ground and saw the sea of lightning patches drifting further away behind us.

"Old pirate trick," grinned Jackson. "You can use lightning to make your ship go faster."

The thunder storm behind us crackled and roared, like a malevolent god laughing at our own inevitable doom.

12

I woke up in my captain's quarters to a bright ray of sunshine coming through the windows. Serena laid in bed beside me, still asleep. Weren't first mates meant to be up before the boss? I smiled. I didn't mind if she rested all day. It wasn't easy telling me about her past. It wasn't easy living through painful memories all over again.

I rolled out of bed and got dressed. I took a quick scan of the ship's stats.

Horizon's Dream

Type: Air Frigate
Size: Large
Turning Radius: Wide
Classification: Warship
Min. Crew: 16
Crew: 33/200
Cannon(s): 14/32
Cargo: 45/80 (tonnage)
Speed: Fast

Crystal Mana Fuel: 178%

Food Supply: High
Health: 90% (Good)
Crew Morale: Happy
Gold: 10,000

As things usually went on these types of journeys, all of the stats were falling, but the positive news was they weren't falling by much. The crew morale had dropped because of the thunderstorm, but was still in the positive rankings. Health and fuel had taken a hit, which was to be expected.

Out on the deck, I found the crew already at work. Many of them tying knots on the yards or staring out into the beautiful blue sky from the rope ladders. The two moons of Illyria were faded circles, watching over us from up high in the sky.

Jackson stood on the side of the quarterdeck, admiring the calm sight of the cloud ocean. He sipped on a mug of coffee.

"Morning captain," he said when I approached. "Wanna cup?"

"Sure."

He had a mug waiting for me. He picked it up and with a metal thermos poured me some coffee. It was still hot and fresh. It tasted good against the breeze of the cloud ocean.

"We've reefed the sails to maximize our speed with the wind, while slowing down the mana engine to stay on top of fuel," explained Jackson.

"Sounds good. How far are we from La-Archanum?"

"At the rate we're currently going, we will be there in about a day's time."

"Have you ever been to La-Archanum? I can't imagine what it would be like. A floating city in the clouds."

"I was there briefly, *once*," said Jackson. "Wouldn't say I was a fan. The place is rowdy and run by sky pirates. A bit of a shit show if you ask me."

"I'm still curious to see it," I said, taking a sip from my mug. I was happy to hear things were going okay for us so far. We were making good time.

"What are we going to do for the rest of the day?"

"All we can do is wait and hope the wind keeps blowing in the direction we want and nothing comes to harm us. The best thing we can do is catch lunch and extra fish to sell to the sky pirates when we arrive."

Jackson waddled over to the side and came back with two skyrods. "Have you ever skyfished before?"

I shook my head and he handed me a rod. I gripped the rod and a message appeared in my HUD.

Introduction to Skyfishing

Skyfishing is a great way to pass the time while travelling through the cloud oceans of Illyria. Skyfish can be used for healing and nourishment buffs, improving crew morale by adding to the ship's food storage, and can also be sold to merchants and vendors.

Skyfishing is a skill that can be leveled up like all other similar crafting, gathering, and professional skills.

I turned the skyrod over in my hand. It was the combination of an actual fishing rod, a harpoon gun, and a kite. A sharp metal blade rested at the top of the rod with two sturdy cloth wings attached to it. Beneath the winged blade was a hook for bait. This contraption was tied to a clear lining attached to a spinning reel. The bottom portion of the rod curved like a revolver offering a grip and trigger for launching the blade.

"First you hold it up to the sky like a rifle," said Jackson, holding his skyrod and pointing it upward into the clouds. "Then you pull the trigger, see."

The bladed kite shot into the air, dragging the lining of the rod with it, up into the clouds. It eventually stopped and floated in the air very much like a normal kite.

"At this point, you change the way you hold it and your hand positions," explained Jackson further. He gripped the reel with one hand and held the rod with the other, much like you would when normal fishing. "And now—the most glorious part of fishing—*you wait*."

"I've never heard anyone describe *waiting* so enthusiastically," I said.

The old Rorn fighter laughed and wiped his eye. "My son used to say the same thing." The brawler gestured towards the skyrod. "Go on, then. *Try it*."

I lifted the skyrod to the clouds. "Where am I aiming it?"

"Into the clouds, boy!"

"Whatever you say," I said, pulling the trigger. The butt of the gun knocked into my shoulder as the hooked blade shot off into the clouds. I followed Jackson's instructions and readjusted my position, gripping the rod and spinner, ready to reel in whatever bites the rod.

I stood there for about a minute and remembered why I never fished back IRL. Because it was boring beyond belief. I remained there as the crew around us readjusted the sails to meet the wind, waiting for something to happen. Anything.

I adjusted my stance, ready to reel the line in defeat,

when the faintest nudge tugged on my rod. A bite. My rod bent upwards as whatever caught hold of my line ripped ferociously at the hook. I reached for the spinner. I pulled across the deck.

"You got it, kid," said Jackson.

I reeled and reeled. Out in the sky was a floating red fish with glowing orange scales, violently tugging at the hook. I reeled and pulled the line back. The fish dangled and squirmed from the top of my rod.

A notice appeared in my HUD.

Congratulations! You caught a sun kelp! Size: 12 cm.
Rating: C-class.

You increased your skyfishing skills by 0.4

I removed the fish from the line. It was no longer squirming. Once the message came on, the fish had become mine. The skyfish flopped around for a bit on the deck, until I dematerialized it into my inventory.

"I guess we know what's for lunch today," said Shade, stepping onto the quarterdeck and giving me a congratulatory pat on the back.

"Let's not limit our options," said Jackson. "Look around."

We passed through a puff of clouds and came upon a stretch of sky filled with schools of skyfish. Floating crabs twisted and turned, while neon green bubble fish floated through the air. A whole set of twenty or thirty bright yellow fish flew through the sky in unison. Blue skyhorses spun and flipped through the air. Pink jellyfish pleasantly drifted along.

"Where are we?" I asked.

"It's called a cloud reef," said Jackson. "All the oceans have them. This is one of many in Argon's Rage. They're relatively peaceful pockets of sky ocean where there's less thunder and activity, making it safer for the skyfish to live and swim through the air here."

"It's incredible," said Shade. "I want to *eat them all*."

We all laughed. Jackson handed Shade his rod and went down into the ship's hull to grab more. Kari and Serena joined us and we had a morning of skyfishing. After an hour and a half we'd caught fifteen sun kelp, twelve blue skyhorses, and three skycrab. Five of our catches had been class-A and the rest had been class-B. The reef was clearly only producing high-quality skyfish. We all agreed to store away the class-A fish and half of the class-B fish to sell at La-Archanum when we got there. The rest would be lunch.

Serena and Jackson brought tables from below to the deck's surface, while Shade and Kari worked on setting the table. I was assigned cooking duty. I stood by myself below deck in the ship's kitchen. The pans and utensils called out to me. I had to make a delicious meal. Why hadn't I hired a cook again?

The ship's kitchen had a working stove and grill, with an air vent leading to the top deck. A metal rack held different jars of spices. There was salt, pepper, basil, and oregano along with a few others I recognized. There were also exotic violet leaves and pink powder.

One of the ship's stewards ran down to the hold and brought me butter, onions, and bread. When he got back, I handed him a knife and ordered him to slice the bread. I threw a good scoop of butter into a wok to melt. Next I finely chopped the onions and threw them into the wok as well. I chopped the carrots into rounds and roughly chopped the broccoli into good-sized chunks. Then I materialized the fish and cut them up too.

I threw everything together into the wok and turned to the steward. "Tell me we have soy sauce in the hold?"

"Yes," nodded the steward and ran off. He came back with a large industrial-sized bottle of soy sauce. The kind you only ever saw sold at massive outlets on the freeway or in the kitchens of large restaurants. *Perfect.*

I took the bottle and drenched my frying vegetables and fish with the dark salty sauce. A notice soon appeared in my HUD.

You discovered a new recipe: Skyfish Stirfry
Ingredients: Butter, Onion, Carrot, Broccoli, Sunkelp,
Skyhorse, Skycrab, and Soy Sauce
Skyfish Stirfry improves your skyfishing skills by 10% as well as 5% increased damage to all airborne creatures (Duration: 30 minutes)

Your cooking skills increased by 1.5
You've leveled up Cooking (craft) to Level 4

The steward and I carefully carried the large steaming wok up to the main deck.

Serena, Shade, Kari, and Jackson were all sitting at a long row of tables. The rest of the crew was sitting there too. Serena used a ladle to serve everyone a bowl. Everyone ate and spoke and occasionally looked up to the world of clouds above us and the schools of different sky creatures. For a brief moment, I forgot we were on a deadly mission or that we were racing against a foreign super power out to destroy us or that the odds of us succeeding weren't very high. For a brief second, I relaxed. I played footsy with Serena, joked with Shade and Kari, asked Jackson questions about the cloud ocean around us and felt at one with the world around me.

Even I knew the moment couldn't last forever.

Our ship vibrated. Everybody stood up, ready to act.

"What was that?" asked Kari.

Serena pointed ahead and everyone's mouths gaped.

It was a sky squid as big as our ship.

13

Everyone stood up from the table. The crew ran to the rope ladders and climbed up the ship, adjusting the sails. We were currently heading straight in the direction of the alarming creature. It had wet white skin from its fin to the bottom of its mantle. It was angled in such a way we only saw one of its bulbous purple eyes. Its long slippery tentacles weaved in and out of the air like seaweed tendrils. Pink suckers lined the bottom side of the squid's multiple arms. Its stats appeared in my HUD.

Ologos
Level 25
HP: 1280
MP: 28

The mana engine was burning at a low rate, so we were coasting through the air at a gentle pace. We were about a minute away from the bowsprit poking the squid right in the eye.

"Is it about to attack us?" said Kari, gripping her small healer's staff.

"I'm not sure," said Shade, reaching down for the revolvers at his waist.

"My guess is it's upset we ate its dinner," said Serena, reaching for her sword. "I bet it really likes sun kelp."

"Or is it jealous about the tasty smell of my stir-fry and saddened to know it will never eat a meal so delicious?" I chimed. "It's the sad depressing truth about having so many tentacle arms and no cooking utensils."

"Chill out master chef," said Serena. "The stew was good, but not so good as to cause a giant sky monster to have an existential crisis."

Shade turned to Kari. "Was that an example of a 'burn' you've been telling me about?"

I turned to Jackson. "You're the most adept sky adventurer amongst us. What do you think?"

"Everyone remain calm," he said, walking slowly back towards the ship's steering wheel and mana engine. "There's no reason we need to fight this thing."

The stout Rorn man grabbed hold of the ship's steering wheel, adjusted the rudders and angled the ship away from the squid.

We all stood on the deck, cautious and ready for battle, as we slowly drifted across the sky.

"Now we'll crank the engine," said Jackson, "And escape this monstrosity—"

A tentacle arm blasted out from its mouth, stretching out across the sky, and wrapping its arm around the mainmast of our ship. The tentacle coiled around the wooden pole, its pink suckers suctioned themselves to it.

The ship stalled. The engine let out mana exhaust fumes

but we didn't move. We were stuck. The tentacle clutching our ship, clenched and throbbed. The arm was pulling us back towards the squid and the dark abyss of its mouth. Between the slithering tentacles I saw its insides, how its mouth was a circle of sharp tiny teeth followed by a smaller ring of teeth and so on and so forth. A kaleidoscopic meat grinder.

"Jackson—can we crank the engine, rip its tentacle out?"

"I don't think so, mate," said the helmsman. "It's too great a risk to the ship. We're better off facing this thing head on. If it wants a fight, let's give it to him."

"Load the cannons," I yelled across the deck. Crew members shuffled below and I heard the sounds of the cannons being readied. "On count of three," I ordered. "One, two, *three!*"

The ship shook as the ignited cannons fired their massive metal bullets across the sky into the mantle of the squid. Black smoke leaked from the hull of our ship and around the body of the Ologos squid. The smoke cleared. The monster had taken zero damage.

What the—?

"Turrets are ready," shouted one of the crew.

"Unleash turret fire," I yelled.

A wave of laser blasts slammed into the side of the squid. The squid took no damage again.

"Aim for a weak spot," I said. "Shoot its eye!"

The two crew members operating the turrets at the front of the ship, re-aimed their guns and fired again at the big purple eye of the squid. As the laser flew across the sky, the monster raised a tentacle arm, blocking the attack.

Shade slid across the wooden platform of the deck, getting cover from the balustrade at the side of the ship. Peeking over, he fired off rounds from his pistol. The bullet punctured the skin of the squid but bounced off it.

"None of our attacks are doing anything," said the Lirana, ducking for cover. "I think it's immune to purely physical attacks."

The squid let out a horrible wail, followed by a burp of oily black muck flying across the air and splattering across our deck. The black muck was slippery and poisonous. Crewmen screamed as the liquid entered their bloodstream. Kari rushed over to them, stepping around the muck and sending orbs of healing at all the crew members.

I stretched my arms out and triggered air blast, sweeping off the black muck from the deck. Next I shot out a quick water blast to get the final residue of the squid's poison attack off the deck.

The squid flung another tentacle towards us. Jackson jumped in the air and did a spinning backflip kick at the incoming arm. The tentacle recoiled and pulled back towards the safety of the squid's main body.

Two more tentacles flew at us and Jackson jumped in the air and kicked one. He ricocheted off it, heading towards the other with a flaming fist but he was too slow. The tentacle grabbed one of the crew members, wrapping itself around his stomach.

"It won't let go," the crewman screamed. "I can't get out."

His screams became indecipherable as the tentacle dragged the man out into the clouds. The squid brought the sailor to its mouth and ripped off his head like chewing on a tough slab of beef jerky.

The battle was not going well. We needed to play offensively.

"Let's stop waiting for this thing to attack us," yelled Serena running to the edge of the ship. "Let's take the battle to it!"

Serena jumped off the ship towards the monster. Her

blade soldier class came with loads of acrobatic jump abilities quite similar to my own mana puddles. Her jumps allowed her to ricochet off the air so long as her stamina bar was high enough.

Serena jumped and flipped through the air, landing on top of the squid's bone white mantle. She slid down it towards the top of its head, where its eyes were and the tentacles sprouted out from. She lifted her sword and swung down on the monster's gelatinous purple eyeball.

Here comes the damage. Let the critical hit messages stack!

Serena's blade slammed into the eyelid, squishing it like a pillow. Serena pulled away and the eye returned to normal; the sword hadn't punctured the gelatinous surface or dealt any damage at all.

Even the eye was immune to physical attacks?

I whipped fireball after fireball at the squid, but the tentacles simply slashed them in the air, cancelling their attack. Damn—did magic not work against this thing either?

I stretched out my hands and focused on the head of the squid where Serena was standing and cast flame wall. A stretch of flames ran across the head of the monster.

"Serena," I yelled. "Slash your blade through my flame wall *then attack!*"

The blade soldier nodded her head and got to work. She did a crushing blow attack, slamming down on the Ologos with all of her might. The blade travelled through the air, my flame wall, and then the squid's flesh.

Critical hit!

A chunk of HP fell off the Ologos and it wailed and squirmed with angry frustration. Serena unleashed her strike combo next: a series of jabs with her sword getting more and more intense with each attack, culminating in a mega crushing blow. Her sword burned with a fiery brilliance.

The tentacle wrapped around the mainmast of the *Horizon's Dream* uncurled, letting go of the ship as its tentacles went after Serena. Bright golden orbs flew out from Kari's small fox hands, leaving buffs and protect spells on Serena as she became the squid's central target.

It hadn't completely forgotten about the ship though. A tentacle smashed into the hull, dealing damage to the ship's health.

"It's no longer keeping hold of us," shouted Jackson. "Now is our time to *escape*."

"Crank the mana engine," I yelled back to him. I hollered out to Serena. "Get back, we're making our escape."

Serena front flipped off the squid, jumping across the tentacles, making her way back to the deck. Once she was aboard, Jackson cranked the mana engine to full blast. The surviving crew tilted the yards and adjusted the sails. We zoomed off through the clouds, the tentacles of the squid chasing after us.

Each tentacle slowly gave up, except for one. The arm stretched and punched the back of our ship, damaging the mana thrusters.

The ship shook and tremored. My teeth chattered from the intensity of the turbulence. The ship descended into the clouds.

"What's happening?"

"The dented thruster is alternating our course," said Jackson. "We have a big problem guys. We're fucked."

The squid had gone off in a new direction in search of other prey. It was somewhat hard to believe given where we were minutes ago, but the squid was now the least of our worries.

I turned back around and saw our ship heading straight towards a swirl of violent purple lightning. We were not going to be able to exploit this to make us go faster.

The lightning struck the deck, shattering the wood. Jackson held onto the steering wheel but I didn't think it was making a difference. Our ship descended into the dark depths of the cloud ocean.

14

I woke up to the smell of stone and dirt. My head ached while a cold hardness pushed against my cheek. I found myself lying on a cliff face, my head resting against stone. Smoke and debris floated through the air. The smell of ash filled my nostrils. My throat burned. A message appeared in my HUD.

Death's Punishment (Debuff): You feel the horror and pain of death. You lose all EXP gained towards your next level (373 EXP). You gain 30% less EXP on kills (Duration: 6 hours). All ATKP and MTKP damage reduced by 10% (Duration: 6 hours). HP and MP regeneration 10% slower (Duration: 6 hours).

Ugh. I had died. The memory of my death was already fading away, the pain and horror replaced by the simple rational fact I had died and come back. This was the fifth time I'd died in the game since entering it. I had been stabbed to death by a corrupted glitch-fueled rat creature, decapitated by the king's most loyal advisor, splattered on

the ground after an airship accident, mauled apart by ferocious sabre tooth tigers, and now splattered to the ground
from an airship accident a second time.

I faintly recalled the blank nothingness of dying in
Arcane Kingdom Online but even now, waking up seconds
after my fifth death, it was already more of an abstract idea
than anything else. I knew death was horrible and I never
wanted to experience it; the comfort of knowing I'd come
back didn't make it easier. Would I eventually hit a limit
where I'd start remembering the deaths, the pain, the awful-
ness? How many times did you have to die in this game
before it really messed you up psychologically? What about
those players enslaved by Arethkar? How traumatized and
screwed up in the head were they after having lost control of
their avatars for so long?

I rolled over and rubbed my eyes. I sat up on the ground
and took in my surroundings. A smashed-up *Horizon's
Dream* lied entrenched in the ground from its crash landing.
Black smoke emanated through the cracked wood of the
deck. I jumped up and ran to the ship. Wood split and
cracked across the deck and smoke emanated from the
inside. I climbed up and went below deck and found the
small remnants of a fire. I stretched out my arms and cast
water blast, taking care of the flames.

I leaned my head against the wall, sighing. The ship was
badly busted up; I had to stop it from getting any more
destroyed if we hoped of ever getting out of here. Wherever
this was.

I checked my HUD to view the ship's stats.

Horizon's Dream

Type: Air Frigate

Size: Large
Turning Radius: Wide
Classification: Warship
Min. Crew: 16
Crew: 18/200
Cannon(s): 14/32
Cargo: 45/80 (tonnage)
Speed: Fast
Crystal Mana Fuel: 0% (Empty)

Food Supply: High
Health: 15% (Bad)
Crew Morale: Defiant
Gold: 10,000

If the burning wreck of a ship in front of me wasn't enough to sink my spirits, the updated stats of the ship were. Holy fuck. The engine had busted, sending our crystal mana fuel down to 0%. The ship's health was in the red. The crew morale had dropped by several notches, which was unsurprising, since we now had barely the minimum crew members to operate the ship. We had lost fifteen men to the crash.

My stomach churned. Energy drained out of my body. My chest became heavy. My legs wobbled unable to stand straight.

The giant pit of guilt was eating me alive from the inside out.

I had made the decision to go with the faster route to beat Arethkar to Ariellum. I had chosen to go through this dangerous path and look where it had gotten my crew and me. In my desperation to beat General Oren Kaige—to save Land's Shield, to protect those I loved—I'd ended up hurting myself and others more than if I had done nothing at all.

No. I shook my head. The crew's blood wasn't on my hands. Their deaths weren't my fault. We were the last hope between our current Illyrian world order and a way worse one dictated by Arethkar. We had to do everything in our power to stop them.

I snapped out of my thoughts and climbed out from below the ship. Beyond the cliff face I'd respawned on was a jungle of palm trees and exotic plants. The silhouette of a mountain loomed in the distance. Emerging from the trees were two familiar faces. Shade and Kari ran up to me.

"Clay, you're back," said Kari. "We weren't sure if you'd respawn on the island or—"

She didn't have to finish her sentence. We still weren't sure what happened if you died falling from the cloud ocean. Did you respawn on the most recent grounded location? Or did you continuously respawn there in an endless loop? I figured the developers wouldn't let the latter be the case, but then again, it wasn't something you wanted to test and find out. Also, the developers—including the mysterious creator Konrad Takeshimi—had proven themselves to be absolute psychopaths again and again in terms of design decisions.

"What happened?"

"We went straight into a lightning swirl and the ship fell," said Shade. "I thought we were done for. This was it. Sayonara Shade. It's been fun but it's all over now. But alas —oh thankfully alas!—Kari held onto me, casting protect and heal over and over so when we crash landed on here we stayed alive with a few scraps of HP between us. Most of the crew wasn't so lucky."

My stomach lurched with guilt again.

"Where are we even? I thought the cloud ocean was an endless expanse of open air."

"For the most part, yeah," said Shade. "But the great rift wasn't so neat and tidy, pockets of Illyria separated completely from the main continents, forming sky islands dotting all across the cloud oceans."

"I learned that at the academy," added Kari. "The Muumuu isles to the east are a whole cluster of islands like this, rather than a giant slab of land like Laergard and Arethkar."

"Does this place have a name or inhabitants?" I said, peering into the jungle, searching for signs of life. A new message popped up in my HUD.

New discovery! Zeratha's Isle
You have discovered Zeratha's Isle. Recorded in history books, its exact location has puzzled cartographers and sky sailors for centuries! The coordinates have been recorded into your captain's logs. Submit them to a skyfarer's guild in any major Illyrian city and collect a reward!

"Anyone else seeing this message?"

"I am," said Kari.

Shade nodded as well. "Great news for us—that is, if we ever get off this bloody island. A discovery like this will net us a mountain of gold coins."

The crew morale in my HUD bounced from defiant to unhappy. The prospect of more gold even in dire straights was enough to raise people's spirits just a little.

"Jackson! Serena!" yelled Kari, pointing behind me.

I turned around. The two had both materialized on the cliff face. My shoulders fell and the pit of guilt in my stomach faded. I wiped my eye and ran towards them. I hugged Serena first. She whispered in my ear, "Looks like shortcuts can be dangerous."

"I'm just happy you're okay."

"Me too," she said. "I mean, I'm happy you're okay. I mean, I'm happy we're both okay."

We laughed. It wasn't a happy occasion or a moment where laughter was anywhere near appropriate, but we laughed anyway.

Jackson scratched the back of his head. He stared out into the distance, not talking, looking over the ship stats straightaway. He headed over to the ship and poked around. When he came back, I asked him, "What do you think?"

We waited for his response with trepidation.

"The mana engine is busted but I think I can fix it. We'll need to chop down wood and repair the deck. We won't be able to get the ship back up to 100% health but we can get it to a functional state. We still have one last problem though: we lost all the crystal mana fuel."

We sighed and dropped our heads. There was no hope for us then. We were stuck on this island. We better make an SOS sign.

"*But*," said Jackson raising a pudgy index finger up like a school teacher. "By its very nature, this floating island stays afloat by its natural crystal mana deposits at the core of its foundations. If we find the core, we will be able to mine enough crystal mana to get us back on track to La-Archanum."

We all nodded our heads, including the crew sitting off by themselves. We were making a plan. Hope was not lost.

"So the question is," continued Jackson, looking out into the shadowy jungle of the floating sky island. "Who stays here with me and who delves into the unknown?"

Serena slashed her giant sword like a machete, cutting a path for us through the floating island's jungle. Thick bushes and leaves came up to our waists, making traversal incredibly difficult. The place was clearly uninhabited. It was sticky and humid the deeper into the jungle we went. While Jackson and the remaining crew members stayed back at the cliff repairing the ship—Serena, Shade, Kari, and I had left on the mining expedition.

"Are we sure we'll be able to find our way back," said Kari, looking up and around at the shadows of the trees, nervously.

Serena stopped and glanced back at the path we had made. "There's only one discernible path on this island and we've made it. I think we'll be fine."

"Sheesh," said Shade scratching the back of his head. "I can't say I've ever been in a hurry to go to *La-Archanum*."

"Have you ever been?" I asked.

"No, but I know many who have. Let's just say there's acquaintances there I don't care to see."

"AKA, people you swindled at cards," joked Serena.

rocks. The cripple and burning debuffs whittle away its remaining HP and it died fully barbequed.

+122 EXP!

Serena turned to me. "And here I thought I was going to finish it off."

I snapped my fingers like a magician. "What can I say—I got tricks up my sleeve."

A wailing groan came from across the clearing. "How about you say: Let's help Shade, he's the only poor sap fighting the biggest monster here!"

Shade was kiting magnificently, but the creature's eyes were glowing red and wising up to Shade's movements, attempting to psyche him out and outmaneuver him.

"Let me take over," said Serena running straight into the battle. She leapt and landed in a smash attack. The crystalladon curled up, leaving no fleshy bits exposed; only glowing crystallized armor. Serena's sword clinked against the monster's defenses.

"Argh!" Serena groaned. She knocked her sword against the shell, not inflicting any damage.

Shade ran up to it and did a spinning dual-wield dagger move. He didn't make a scratch.

I triggered Earthquake again followed up with molten fireballs to heat up the ground. The defensive crystalladon rumbled and shook from its shielded core. Its HP dwindled more and more.

"What happens when it reaches zero?" asked Kari, concerned.

"Uh oh," I said, running towards the trees. "Take cover, it's about to blow!"

The scales of the crystalladon blast across the clearing, digging into the nearby trees and ground.

I stood up from the bush I was hiding behind and took in the empty clearing. I scanned the clear blue crystal stuck to one of the trees.

New Item Alert
Bit of Crystallized Mana (x1)

I pulled the bit out and examined it further.

Bit of Crystallized Mana (x1)
Combine with three other bits to form a Shard of Crystallized Mana

We scavenged the clearing, picking up more bits of crystallized mana. About seven of them came from the large crystalladon. The remaining pieces of scale were normal scales. I added them to my inventory as well.

I crouched over the fallen crystalladons and scanned them for items. I got messages for more bits of crystallized mana. I materialized my sword and cut off the glowing blue bits from the creature's scales.

"I think the mana engine runs on shards rather than bits," said Serena. "Do we have any idea how many more Shards we need?"

I shot a quick party message to Jackson telling him the good news about finding monsters that dropped crystal mana as well as asking how many shards we needed.

Jackson: We need to get the engine back to 70% if we want to get to La-Archanum safely. I can't say

for sure, but I believe we will need, at least, 82 shards or more.

It wasn't going to be easy. 82 shards meant we had to get 328 bits of crystallized mana. We had a big day ahead of us.

"Let's go hunt more crystalladons gang!"

We rummaged through the forest for another half an hour and came across nothing but insects.

"Was that the last of the crystalladons then?" asked Kari.

"They'll respawn any minute," said Serena, clutching the hilt of her sword.

We continued through the jungle. Sweat formed on my brow as the panic settled in. What if there were no more crystalladons? Would we have to dig a hole to the center of this island? Then the jungle cleared and a stone mound with an open doorway, leading underground, beckoned us to approach.

A dungeon crypt.

I peered into the darkness. I had a strong feeling crystal mana deposits would be down there.

But what else awaited in the darkness?

16

We went down a dark mounded path of dirt. We walked and walked. We went so deep we were surrounded by darkness. It was so dark I had to be careful with every step. I summoned a fireball in my hands, illuminating the passage.

"I knew your class was good for something," teased Serena.

"*Hey*—next time I cook, I'll get you and your massive blade to chop the onions. Put you to real work."

Serena laughed. "Okay, deal."

We walked down the dark winding tunnel until the ground at our feet glowed with pink and blue lines. Crystallized mana at our feet. The passage we'd been walking on opened up into a wide open cavern, brightly lit with giant mounds of crystals. Shards poked out of the ground like diamond flowerbeds. The shards were massive; as big as the quarterdeck of our ship.

All along the winding path were crystalladons walking back and forth, sniffing the ground, kicking up dirt. Glowing slime stalactites hung from up above in the high echelons of the caverns ceiling. Bats fluttered up top.

"Where are we?"

"We must be pretty close to the crystal core of the island," said Shade. "A floating island like this will have a reservoir of crystal mana at its center. They say the mana deposits at the bottom of a continent like Laergard stretch on for full valleys." Shade glanced around the cavern again, his nose twitching. "This is quite a bit of crystal mana. We have to consider not cashing in on the discovery of this island to anyone. These crystals will stay as ours for the taking!"

"How do we even mine them?" asked Serena. "Do we go up to those giant shards with our pickaxes?"

Shade laughed. "I doubt any of our mining skills will be high enough level to do such advanced level gathering. Plus our basic iron pickaxes aren't the highest quality either. No. What we want to find are crystal nodes. They'd be good sources of crystal mana for us to mine."

We stood where we were and scanned the cavern. Across the path closest to us was a little mound. It popped up with its own stat screen.

Small Crystal Node

"I see one," I said.

I ran out to it but Serena put her hand on my shoulder and held me in place.

"Hold on," she said. "Those crystalladons are not going to let us simply mine in front of them, are they?"

Shade shook his head.

"I thought so," said Serena. "Let's take out the two in front of the nearby node and then see what happens when we mine it."

"Okay you're right," I said. "I don't know why but I'm so excited to mine."

"It's because you're a greedy materialist hoarder who likes collecting stuff," said Serena.

"You are throwing me so much shade! Speaking of Shade, I feel like you're describing him, not me."

The rogue coughed. "You see I collect stuff and then I sell it. You keep stuff and leave it in your inventory to potentially 'craft' later."

I crossed my arms. "You guys are haters. That's what you are. Let's take out these crystalladons."

We followed our typical formation. Serena ran in, drawing the aggro of the two monsters while Kari buffed her. Shade attacked the monsters at their rear, digging his knives into their exposed bits of flesh. I brought the destruction altogether with an earthquake plus fireblast combo. A molten earthquake.

+122 EXP!
+122 EXP!

We looted the fallen monsters and gained more bits of crystallized mana.

I headed over to the small crystal node and materialized an iron pickaxe from my inventory. I raised the pickaxe and with all my might stabbed it into the crystal mining node. My arms stung with pain. The pickaxe barely dented the mining node.

Mining attempt failed
Your mining skill increased by 0.1

I turned to the group and they were all laughing at me.

"What the hell!?"

Serena looked to Shade. "I already made fun of his hoarding. Can you explain this to him?"

Shade shook his head and wagged his tail. "Clay—you're not the most physical of classes, so it only stands to reason you wouldn't be very good at mining."

Damn. Some games separated the gathering skills differently from everything else but I guess it wasn't the case here. While attack power didn't directly correlate to my overall strength (which was a combo of ATKP, TGH, and natural muscle) it *was* a major deciding factor; having low ATKP—as I did—was a pretty good indicator of having a low overall level of strength.

"Don't worry though," said Shade. "You can still help. As you mine, your level will increase and so will your ability to mine efficiently despite your low strength."

"Watch how it's done," said Serena, materializing an iron pickaxe in her hands. She stepped in front of the crystal mining node like a baseball batter coming up to the plate. She widened her legs and bent her knees. She pulled the pickaxe back and then knocked it into the node. It made a snapping sound and little bits of crystal fell onto the ground at our feet. I scanned them and they were all coming up as "Bits of Crystallized Mana (xi)". Serena went a full minute, picking at the node. She distilled twenty bits. On her twenty-first swing, her pickaxe crashed into the stone ground. The node had faded away, dematerialized into nothing.

"Huh?"

"We have to wait for this node to respawn or find another one until then."

Geeze. They didn't make mining easy or very efficient, but that was the point. Also, I'm sure if we leveled up our mining skills enough, we'd be able to mine faster and distill more material from each node.

"Look down there," said Kari, pointing to a big open circle full of crystal mining nodes. Another group of five crystalladons waited for us down there.

"Alright," I said. "We know the drill."

Serena ran into tank. Shade attacked from the rear. Kari threw out buffs and offensive blasts from the back. I did crowd control, casting lightning cage to paralyze the crystalladons and keep them at bay so they didn't completely overwhelm Serena. The blade soldier unleashed her blade tornado ability, spinning between the attacking crystalladons, knocking a whole bunch of them over. Shade jumped on the lopsided creatures straightaway, throwing down dagger attacks into their exposed underbellies.

+122 EXP!
+122 EXP!
+122 EXP!
+122 EXP!
+122 EXP!

The area was cleared, leaving six nodes for us to mine on our own.

"Okay guys," I said. "Let's all spread out and take a node for our selves."

Everyone nodded and materialized their iron pickaxes and headed off to work.

I approached my node with new resolve. I always enjoyed gathering materials in games and I didn't want my weak physical stats to screw me out of mining. I lifted up my pickaxe and dug it into the node.

Mining attempt failed
Your mining skill increased by 0.1

I took a deep breath and then lifted my pickaxe again. I threw it down into the node and faced the same message in my HUD.

Mining attempt failed
Your mining skill increased by 0.1

I did this about seven more times, grunting and groaning along with the rest of my party. Kari had a disconcerted look on her face. She was struggling similar to me.

I lifted my pickaxe for a ninth time. I slammed it down into the node and felt the metal pick puncture the surface of the node.

Mining success!
Your mining skill increased by 0.4
Your mining skill has leveled up! (Level 2)

I crouched down and picked up three bits of crystallized mana. Shit. At the rate we were going this was going to take all day. Potentially longer, if there weren't any more nodes.

We each moved onto another node when we depleted one. We mined to the music of our grunts and groans. I was halfway to leveling up my skill again when Kari screamed.

A crystalladon materialized out of nowhere and rammed right into her, taking out half of her HP. Serena ran towards the healer, dematerializing her pickaxe. She then pulled her sword out from behind her back. She stunned the beast with her first attack, then kicked it over and stabbed it to death.

+122 EXP

"Thanks," said Kari, wiping sweat off her forehead. "That was a close one. I guess we have to worry about the crystalladons respawning in here as well."

Serena looked around. "It looks like we've mined most of the nodes here. I say we take a quick break, fight off any more respawning creatures and then continue down the cavern."

"Good," I said. "I have a great break plan as well."

I scanned my inventory and materialized a random stick and a slab of crystalladon meat. Next I punctured the slab of meat with the stick and held it up in the air. With my other hand, I conjured a fireball and held it beneath the slab of meat. The meat sweated and crackled.

Your cooking skill increased by 0.2

I grinned, watching the slab of meat glaze over. It reminded me of a kid when my family and I went camping. Sitting around the fire roasting hot dogs. I smiled, focusing on the similarities rather than the glaring differences.

The group all smiled at my ingeniousness.

"That's right," I said. "Clay Hopewell: human barbeque. Who wants a cooked slab of crystalladon meat?"

Everyone's eyes brightened up at the idea. The smell of the cooked meat was making my mouth water. I wasn't sure how I was supposed to tell when the meat was fully cooked and edible but then I got a message in my HUD.

You discovered a new recipe: Barbequed Crystalladon Meat
Ingredients: Slab of Crystalladon Meat (x1)

Barbequed Crystalladon improves your mining skills by
5% (Duration: 30 minutes)

I walked over and handed the stick to Serena.

"Thank you charming chef," she said.

"No problem," I grinned. "But don't for a second think you've escaped chopping duty later."

She laughed and took bite of the meat. "Mmm. Delicious."

"That's not even the best part," I said, firing up another slab to make for Shade and Kari. "Eating it increases your mining skills."

"Fantastic!"

I fed the rest of the team and then made a slab for myself. It was yummy, especially after all the mining. What would the meat taste like once I applied all the spices back on the airship? My stomach grumbled with excitement.

Swallowing her last bit of barbequed crystalladon, Serena said, "It's crazy to think we're going through all of this for the Ultriga Weapon."

"What do you mean?" I asked. "If it were easy to get the Ultriga Weapon someone would've gotten it already."

"No, I mean, let's say we beat Kaige and get the weapon first. What then? Do we use it to annihilate Arethkar? Do we destroy both them along with the enslaved Chosen? They didn't really choose to be there, did they?"

"The Chosen will respawn."

"Will they?" said Serena. "In terms of power level, people talk about this thing in the same vein as the mark on your wrist. Like it has a god-like power."

I swallowed my last bite of meat. "We don't even know what it does yet."

"Sure," said Serena. "I'm only speculating."

She raised good points, especially about the enslaved Chosen. I'm sure some of the NPCs living under Arethkarian rule didn't agree with everything the high council chose for its country. They didn't deserve to perish in a war between nations.

After eating, we continued down into the mine. The nodes hadn't respawned, but more crystalladon had. If we were going to spend our time fighting, it would be better spent in areas with minable nodes.

As we moved along, I received a message in my HUD.

Personal Message: Time's Running Out

We've got new intel. Oren Kaige's fleet of ships are on course for La-Archanum. Where are you?

Theobold

I closed the message in my HUD and relayed it back to the group.

"Damn," said Serena.

"I know," I said. "Our shortcut was meant to give us the advantage, but it looks like we're still playing catch up. We'll have to mine a lot faster if we want to get off this island and back on track."

Everyone nodded and we went back to searching the caverns. We found another large area much like the one we'd mined previously. It was occupied by crystalladon, which we made quick work of. We mined the nodes when a roar came from further down the passage.

I shivered. "What the heck?"

I let the others continue mining as I peered deeper down

into the cavern. In the distance was a large golem with a
massive mana crystal glowing on its back.

Crystal Golem
Level 20
HP: 1130
MP: 29

I hurried back to the group. "Guys! There's a golem
down there with a giant mana crystal on its back. I bet if we
slayed it, we'd get a ton of crystallized mana. Definitely
more then what we've been collecting here so far."

Serena made a face. "I don't think it's in our best interest
to fight such a high level monster. It will only be a couple of
more hours if we mine here."

"You don't know that," I said. "You're assuming the nodes
we mined respawn quickly. We can be out of here and flying
off to La-Archanum in no time if we take the crystal
golem out."

Kari wiped sweat off her eyes and shrugged.

Shade scratched his chin. "I'm not sure about it mate.
The deeper we go into this cavern the more dangerous the
monsters are, even if their levels aren't high. They've lived a
long time, long enough for their skills and ability levels to
far outstrip their base stats. The risk isn't worth it."

I didn't know why the party was so skeptical. Kaige was
getting closer to Ariellum by the second while we were
sitting ducks on a floating island in the middle of nowhere.

"C'mon guys," I said. "When did we ever weigh the risks
like this before? We have a mission to accomplish. One with
a shrinking deadline. Anything that gets us closer to
succeeding at our quest faster has to be done."

"What about the shortcut that landed us here?" said Serena.

Her point hit me like a punch to the gut, but this was different. The squid attack was out of our control; fighting the crystal golem wouldn't be. We knew how to fight in party formation, we were the same level as it, and there were four of us and only one of it.

"I'm going in," I said. I headed down the cavern towards the crystal golem.

The steps of my teammates echoed behind me. They were coming with me, even though they thought I was being impulsive and crazy.

My fingers twitched in prep for a spell.

I would do whatever it took to beat Kaige to Ariellum.

17

The golem walked back and forth, patrolling the open zone of the passage. It had the shape and body of an oversized gorilla, except instead of flesh and fur, it was constructed entirely of crumbled stone. A large pink crystal jutted out from its back, glowing, brightening up the area of the cavern. Such a large mana crystal would surely power our airship to where we needed to go.

"Let me debuff it first," I yelled. I hurried ahead, waving my arms across the ground in front of me. I manipulated the ground below the monster's feet, destroying and tearing it into crumbled dangerous shreds. My palms heated up with molten balls of flame next. I whipped each blast, heating up the destroyed ground, crippling the cavern creature.

The golem yelled out with rage and stretched out an arm of its own, shooting a crystal blast at me. I spun around and faced my teammates, who were looking at me strangely. I smirked and initiated flame dodge, hurling myself towards the monster, leaving a trail of flames beneath my boots. I grimaced at the golem's shard blast shattering against the ground where I'd been standing. I spun around, stretching out my hands, letting a frosty energy exit my body and create a plate of frozen ground behind the golem.

The monster raised a clenched stone fist, high in the air, ready to smash down on me. I electric blinked a few feet away and initiated air blast. A gust of wind blew forth from my hands, pushing the golem onto the frozen ice. It slipped and fell.

Chilled, burning, crippled. Three debuffs flickered beneath the golem's status bars, eating away at its HP. I flame dodged back towards the others, yelling, "Back to normal formation. Go, go, go!"

Serena rushed towards the monster, triggering her charge attack, zigzagging her way closer and closer to the disoriented golem. She landed out of the charge attacks with a crushing blow, drawing on all of her strength and energy to slam her giant sword into the creature's chest. Shards of rock chipped off it like a mining node. Serena yelled and grunted, slashing her sword again and again into the monster.

Shade hurried in behind the beautiful tank warrior, dealing spinning attacks and knife jabs on the creature's rear. Kari threw protect spells at both Serena and Shade, showering them both with golden light.

I stood beside Kari, taking in the battle from the sidelines. I materialized an MP potion from my inventory and uncorked the glass bottle. I guzzled down the blue liquid. It tasted like watered down cough syrup.

The crystal golem raised its fist, preparing its hammer smash. It threw down its clenched fist. Serena met the attack with her sword, holding it up horizontally, blocking the attack with sword shield.

Distracted in its battle of wills, Shade jabbed the monster in the ribs. The crystal golem lifted its other hand

and swiped across the area, knocking Shade back. The thief flew across the cavern. He tumbled and fell to the ground, dropping 35% of his HP.

Kari shot a healing spell his way, a glowing orb flying across the cavern and replenishing Shade's HP to 100%.

I gotta get back in this.

My palms heated up with flame and I whipped one fireball after another at the creature. The balls of flame smashed into the chest of the golem, dealing a blaze of damage.

The crystal golem roared and lifted its fist away from its struggle with Serena. It knocked her to the side and charged towards me.

Uh oh. I'd drawn its hate.

"Protect Kari," yelled Serena, rushing to catch up with the golem and get its aggro back onto her.

I stretched out my arms and initiated air blast, pushing the golem back a step. It wasn't enough to slow the monster's momentum. It stumbled and then continued its charge towards me. Shit. If we lost Kari, we lost our healer and potentially the battle. I clenched my fists and triggered stone skin, getting myself ready to fight the golem one on one. Its fist crashed down towards me. I threw my hand up at the last minute and unleashed lightning cage, disabling the golem's attack.

The golem stumbled, but then returned with a sweep attack. He knocked me over and sent me flying. I smashed into Kari. The fox girl went soaring. I blinked in the air and caught her, falling to the ground, cushioning her fall onto the cavern floor.

I stood up and saw the golem was now fighting Serena again. I materialized another MP potion. I guzzled it down and readied myself to unleash a string of attacks. I rushed towards it, blinked onto its neck. I stretched out both my arms and unleashed skull shock. Electricity burst from each of my finger tips into the head of the crystal golem. Its eyes faded and it spun on its feet.

"Guys, its stunned," I yelled. "This is it. Kill it now."

I cast flame wall in front of the golem, adding burning damage to Serena's and Shade's blade attacks.

I jumped off and triggered earthquake at its feet and lobbed fireballs at the ground.

The creature's HP whittled down to zero, collapsing onto the ground.

+175 EXP!

I ran up to the crystal golem and scanned its body.

New Item(s) Alert!
Crystallized Mana Core (x1)
Crystal Scales (x5)
Rock (x10)

I got to work, sawing off the crystal core from the fallen body. I scanned the item once it was in my inventory and my eyes glowed with happiness.

Crystallized Mana Core = 500 crystallized mana shards

Sweet. This was more than what we needed to power the ship and get back on our mission.

"Look at that," I said. "We did it guys. I told you so."

Shade helped Kari off the ground and Serena gave me a face I hadn't seen since our college days, when I'd show up to work late or talk about not giving a shit about anything.

Her face was full of disappointment, like she wasn't looking at me, but at someone else.

My arms fell to my side, jubilance disappearing by the second. "C'mon guys, why aren't you pumped? We've got the crystal mana needed to get out of here."

The party avoided looking me in the eyes.

No one spoke except Serena.

"Whatever you say, *captain*."

18

Nobody spoke as we walked out of the cavern. The silence between the group was made more painful with the crunch of our boots on pebbles and the whistle of the wind. Things didn't get better even when we exited. We trudged through the jungle path from which we came until we were back by the cliff face and found the *Horizon's Dream* looking brand new.

The wood on the hull and deck gleamed with a shine of freshness. The crew were busy hammering in last minute places, but generally the ship looked fantastic. As we approached, Jackson appeared on the deck and stretched his arms out wide. "Like what you see?"

"How did you fix it so fast?" said Kari, blinking in awe and perplexity.

Jackson crossed his big burly arms and guffawed. His time in the arena had really left him with a penchant for showboating. "Easy. It was a matter of gathering the necessary materials and selecting the proper repair tabs in the menu. Resources weren't an issue—this island has plenty of them."

Silence.

I opened my eyes, awaiting a prompt saying something like, "engine restart failed," but thankfully that wasn't the case. Behind the closed door of the furnace was a bright pink glow of burning mana. The ship rumbled as new energy coursed through it.

I checked in on the stats. Everything had been restored.

Horizon's Dream

Type: Air Frigate
Size: Large
Turning Radius: Wide
Classification: Warship
Min. Crew: 16
Crew: 18/200
Cannon(s): 14/32
Cargo: 45/80 (tonnage)
Speed: Fast
Crystal Mana Fuel: 105%

Food Supply: Medium
Health: 85% (Good)
Crew Morale: Neutral
Gold: 10,000

The fuel levels, ship health, and crew morale were all up. I smiled and closed my HUD.

"Well done kid," said Jackson. "Looks like we're going to be getting out of here."

I leaned back against a wall and sighed. "Phew. It wasn't all for nothing then."

"What wasn't?" said Jackson, lifting his eyebrows in

curiosity again. "Does this have anything to do with the tension I witnessed upstairs?"

I sighed and quickly told him what happened. How the rest of the party didn't want to fight the crystal golem but I insisted and almost got us all killed because of it.

"The thing is," I said. "The crystal golem was worth the risk."

Jackson nodded along with my story. He didn't say anything for a full minute afterwards. We stood there in the rumbling engine room as he thought. He was contemplating something. Picking his words, wondering what he should say, and what he shouldn't.

"I was a boxer," said Jackson. "You know, before entering this game. It's why I naturally found myself playing this brawler class. Anyways, I had a wife and two kids. One boy who was six, a girl who was four. My wife was a nurse and I did a few shifts a week in construction. On my days off I was making a go at working as a semi-professional fighter. Then, one day, my wife got hit by a car. She became paralyzed from the waist down. She was in a wheelchair for life. Our insurance went through the roof. Even as I took more shifts building bridges or whatever the hell needed building—we weren't making enough anymore to take care of all of us. So I made a choice. An executive decision. I reached out to some bad people and we came to an arrangement and I took a dive on a big match."

"You did the right thing, though," I said. "You needed to help your kids and your wife. What else were you supposed to do?"

"I guess," Jackson said, staring at the wall behind me, unable to look me in the eye. He was telling me a small portion of a much larger story. This was just one episode.

Where it all ultimately led, he was holding back and he didn't want me to ask further.

"Here's the thing," said Jackson, continuing with his train of thought. "Each time you rationalize a bad decision, you walk one step closer to the edge."

"The edge of where."

"The abyss."

19

I spent the next part of the journey holed up in my captain's quarters. Jackson occasionally visited to let me know about any updates to our current flight path, changes to the wind or turbulence ahead. I nodded and told him to handle it however he saw fit. I didn't want to go outside and face the torment of my party's silent treatment so I inflicted myself to my own self-imposed exile in my room, away from the rest of my party and crew.

A few hours passed, most of which, I spent either going over my stats, looking over my skill abilities, or contemplating where I wanted to go next with my class. After this quest, Theobold said we would discuss where I'd go next with my build. Currently, I had fulfilled the requirements necessary to unlock the Mage quest trial, but with six class skill points still available for me to spend, I could easily learn the required abilities for whichever class I wanted. At first I thought that made things easy, but when I looked over my skills I realized *yes, I could learn any six spells instantly right now*, but it would lock me out from seven other possible spells at my disposal. I wasn't sure if I'd be able to keep investing class skill points into abilities once upgrading to a tier-2 class. These concerns kept me from spending all my points in an unconstrained shopping spree.

I also wasn't sure where I wanted to go next. Mage would be more of the same but with even cooler moves; but I was curious to unlock one of the more idiosyncratic classes like Summoner or Illusionist. The impatient gamer in me spotted a new button at the bottom of the class menu. "*Initiate Mage Quest Trial*." I wanted to press it so badly to see what happened, but I resisted the urge.

I leaned my head against the walls of the ship as I sat on my bed. I better check-in with Theobold to let him know how our mission was going. I jotted a quick message and sent it over to him. I was about to close my eyes and take a nap when there was a knock on my door.

"Come in," I said.

I expected Jackson but in came Serena.

"Well, this is going to be awkward—what with you not talking to me," I said.

Serena gestured back towards the door and I reached my hands out towards her. "No, wait. What is it? I'm sorry for being a dickhead. It's hard sometimes because it comes so easily and natural to me I don't even realize I'm doing it."

She smirked. "*Tell me about it*."

I got off the bed and walked towards her. "Look: I know you think I was an idiot for fighting the crystal golem back there, but it all worked out, didn't it? And wasn't it you who said I was the one who had to make the hard decisions?"

She nodded her head and I felt like I was both right and wrong at the same time.

"I'm scared," she said. "We're already different from the people we were before entering this game. I'm worried—

with all this fighting, killing, and questing—what will we eventually become, you know?"

I pulled off my gloves and raised my hands. My palms were full of lines and marks. Were they the same palms I had prior to entering this world? I had no way of knowing.

"The people we were outside this game, weren't equipped to live here," I said. "Weren't ready to fight for survival. Yet that's the position we've been placed in and why we have to keep on fighting. We're fighting for the sake of the people we once were and everyone who's come into this game and was unable to step up to the task. Stopping Arethkar, freeing the enslaved Chosen, getting to the bottom of all of these glitches—solving all these problems will help us turn Illyria into more than just a game in which we're fighting to survive, but a place where we can truly *live*."

Serena's blue eyes widened as I spoke. They even sparkled for a second, gleaming with hope. "You really think we can truly make this place a home?"

"Hell if I know. I don't even know what class I want to take next, but we're gonna bloody try," I said.

She stepped closer to me so our bodies touched. She looked up and I down at her. I bent over to kiss her when there was a knock on the door.

"Oi! Lovebirds," shouted Shade. "You're gonna wanna come see this."

Serena fluttered her eyelashes. "Rain check on that kiss?"

I smiled and nodded as she took me by the hand and led me back up to the top deck.

The sky was the faint orange of dusk. Pink clouds rolled through the air. The hum of nearby airship engines echoed across the way and in the distance was a majestic airborne city. A floating spire in the sky. Different docking stations with long runways stretched out from the silver tower, rotating around it in the air. It was a sublime sight: the gears, the propellers, the engines, everything involved in keeping this city afloat. Airships floated around it, a few smaller ones did laps around the structure, racing in the sky. Bright glowing signs of shops on the lower levels of the tower, flickered in the shadows beneath the rotating docks. Rusting pipes near the bottom occasionally released sludge of murky sewage into the endless sea of clouds. Black smoke billowed out from different chimneys and engines from the bottom to the top of the floating city. Everyone on deck stood still, looking out to the place in wonder and amazement.

La-Archanum.

The halfway point in our journey. A lighthouse in the clouds. A beacon of hope. The waypoint to the next leg of our quest.

I eyed the rotating docks, looking at the in and outgoing ships, whether or not any of them sported the red and purple Arethkarian colors. All the ships had their own banners, sailed into the skies for no one but themselves. They were the ships of free agents. Sky pirates.

Two specks glowed out from the dock. The specks grew bigger and bigger until it was clear they were ships heading towards us. They were small silver cruisers. One approached our ship, slowing down at the side of our deck, close enough to chat. The other cruiser hovered back, ready for any surprises from us. On the ship closest to us, stood a tall Lirana man with gray fur and a matching tail. He had a red bandana tied across his head. He wore run-down rags and had a scabbard and pistol hanging from his waist. He turned to us. "Who is the captain of this vessel?"

Everyone looked to me. I nodded my head in assent.

"What business do you have at La-Archanum?"

"We're passing through on a mission for the King of Laergard."

The Lirana pilot glanced at our green banners. "If you wish to dock at La-Archanum, those colors will be an issue. Our home is a free city, belonging to no king or queen. The titles of groundlings mean nothing here. La-Archanum is diplomatically neutral in all Illyrian affairs. You may wear your colors, but you enter as neutral actors."

I ordered a crew member to untie the green Laergardian banners from the ship. I had a quick pang of guilt for the lack of loyalty I was displaying, but these so-called security guards needed to be appeased before they'd let us enter the city.

The Lirana guard nodded at the removed banners. "You may proceed to docking point-b."

The cruiser spun in the air and headed towards the floating sky city as we followed behind.

20

We landed the *Horizon's Dream* onto one of the floating city's docking stations. Muumuu dockworkers waved glowing light sticks to signal where they wanted us to land. Once parked, two Lirana pirate guards approached us. They had red bandanas tied to their heads, their black furry ears poking out from the knotted cloth. Sabers were sheathed to their waist, resting alongside their shaggy breeches.

"Welcome to La-Archanum," said one pirate. "Before you can depart and enter the city's center, you must pay the crystal mana tax."

A message came up on my HUD.

Welcome to La-Archanum
To enter the city, the Horizon's Dream must donate 5% of its total crystallized mana to the ship. Will you donate 5% of your crystal mana: Y/N?

"What? No one told me about this," I said.
"We're telling you now," said the other pirate.

"But we came here to stock up on crystal mana, not give it away," I said.

"And you'll be able to purchase such fuel upon gaining entry to the city," said the original pirate. "The tax is levied on all entrants of La-Archanum to keep our way station of safety and hospitality afloat in this otherwise troubling cloud ocean."

"Pay it," said Jackson, standing behind me. "This city was founded by pirates for this very reason. A toll station across the skies."

The two pirates blinked with disbelief. "Such slander is far from the truth good sir. La-Archanum was founded on the principles of safety and friendly co-operation in this troubling world. Our goal has always been to minimize shipwrecks, disappearances, and deaths across Argon's Rage. Since the city's founding hundreds of years ago—when it was merely a collection of ship's tied together in the air—such horrifying incidents have diminished greatly."

"And you have profited immensely from it," grumbled Shade, joining the conversation.

"Oh, how I wish everyone profited from good deeds," mused the original pirate. "In an ideal world, good deeds are rewarded and bad ones punished, no?"

Kari and Serena laughed.

"What's so funny?" asked the pirate.

"You remind us of another Lirana we know," said Serena, cheeks bright red.

Shade shook his head in disappointment. "We Lirana are natural wordsmiths, yes, but honestly Serena—I thought you held me in higher esteem than these pirates."

"You're a thief," said Kari. "Aren't they the same thing?"

Both Shade and the pirates both spat at the floor with disgust. "Of course not—a thief is—"

together by scraps and junk to create completely unique airships.

At the end of the dock, we entered the city. We were in a circular corridor, one of the rings wrapping around the floating spire. A message came up in my HUD.

You have discovered La-Archanum +100 EXP!

A glowing blue sign said: "Welcome to La-Archanum. Floor-0."

Beneath it was a map showing the city spire. We were in the middle, the landing zone, known as floor-0. The floors were determined by the ringed hallways looping the whole spire. The floors above us went in numerical order, "Floor +1, Floor +2, Floor +3," and below us they were ordered similarly except in the negative, "Floor -1, Floor -2, Floor -3." A glass window wrapped around the ring, showing the final moments of dusk as the sky slowly dimmed. Pink manalamps flickered to give light to the hallways.

The foyer in front of us led to a bustling market full of food stalls and benches. A dark ceiling hung above the area, a metallic black sky. The bleak rooftop was obscured by the smoke from the food stalls. A barbeque station grilled sky-salmon skewers while the stall beside it boiled a yellow curry sauce with sky-prawns and crispy vegetables.

The market was cramped with stalls and people. Rugged Haeren and Rorn soldiers bartered with haggling La-Archanum locals: scraggly gap-toothed merchants selling the usual fare of weapons, armor, and potions with the added selection of rare antiques and treasures from all over the cloud ocean. The different soldiers wore different colors. There was green Laergardian cloth, turquoise for Solmini, and purple for Renzar. There were no soldiers clad with the deep burgundy colors of Arethkar. I sighed with relief.

Lining the market were patches of Lirana. Many of them wore the red bandanas like the pirate guards from earlier. They must be the official city guard then. Beyond them was a noticeable abundance of Lirana: from the guards to the merchants to the beggars sitting on the floor with an open buckets and bottles of whisky beside them. They whispered to each other and glanced suspiciously towards us.

"I feel like we're being watched," I said.

"That's because we are," said Jackson. "La-Archanum is a pirate city, a neutral zone from Illyrian politics, and so, a spy capital."

"There's a saying," said Shade. "*In La-Archanum whispers are as common as the wind.*"

Serena crossed her arms and monitored the different passersby and guards around us. "Who's the boss around here? Who employs the red bandanas?"

"Oh, the Grand Captain Bella, of course," said Shade.

"For someone who's never been here," said Kari. "You know a lot about it."

"Well the Grand Captain Bella and I share a past."

"What kind of past?" asked Kari, pointedly. "Is she a former girlfriend?"

Shade looked off in the distance. "Not quite."

"Can we use your former relationship to help forge a partnership with them?" I asked.

Shade shrugged.

"Okay, we can deal with that later," I said. "We don't have much time to spend. Kaige hasn't docked here yet, so we want to be out of here before he does. Jackson do you wanna go take care of restocking fuel and food on the ship. The rest of you—feel free to sell off your loot and upgrade your gear.

I'm going to go sell those discoveries at the skyfarer's guild and then see if there's been any news about the Arethkarian fleet. Let's meet up after that to form our next plan."

"Sounds good," said Jackson, raising his fingers in a peace sign and walking off.

I left the others and went back to the floor map at the entrance to the floor-o market. The skyfarer's guild was down the hall from where I was standing. I found it tucked away in a narrow alley. The entrance had spinning propellers and a billowing flag with an airship hanging from above. I stepped into a dimly lit building full of maps and scrolls. Glass bottles with miniature frigates and galleons lined the walls. A Haeran man sat at a front desk, slumped over, his bored head slouching into his raised hand as if it were a pillow.

"I'd like to hand in some discoveries," I said. "I hear you purchase them for gold?"

The bored-looking man's eyes perked up at this. "Did you say a discovery?"

"Yeah," I said.

"Yippee," he said, jumping for joy. "We haven't had a discovery here in weeks!"

I was glad to hear. This meant our discoveries would net us more gold. At the same time, it was an odd thing for the man to say. They were a pirate city in the middle of the cloud ocean—surely there were people coming in here with discoveries all the time.

"You're not serious—there must be other skyfarers coming through here?"

The man shook his head. "Nope. Not since the—"

He stopped talking and I glanced at him funny.

"Not since the—? Are you going to finish that sentence?"

The guy smiled and blinked at me. "What sentence? You

mentioned a discovery?" He pulled out a large ledger note-book and placed it front of me. When I focused down on the open book, a message popped up in my screen.

Skyfarer's Guild (La-Archanum Chapter)
Discoveries

Which discoveries would you like to share with the guild today?

Zeratha's Isle – 1,000,000 Gold Coins
Blue Apple – 25,000 Gold Coins
Red Joogu Berries – 25,000 Gold Coins
Crystalladon (species) – 50,000 Gold Coins

I stared dumbfounded at the screen. I was an Illyrian millionaire at the mere press of a button. I wasn't surprised the isle discovery was worth so much. The amount of crystallized mana on the isle was a total gold mine, a cash cow; especially if those crystal golems respawned at a regular rate as well. As I'd thought at the time, the whereabouts of the isle was too good to share with others. Perhaps I'd share it with King Fergus but I definitely didn't want it to be open information on the worldwide stage. Still, handing in the three other discoveries would net us a chunk of change. We'd be able to add new features to the ship as well as raise the morale back to positive. Perfect.

I handed in all the discoveries except for Zeratha's Isle and watched the money rake in onto the ship's status.

I opened up the ship status screen, eager for new upgrades, but nothing appeared. A prompt told me I'd have to be in an aerodrome at a designated upgrade area to alter the ship's equipment. I said goodbye to the guild assistant and returned to the landing bay.

The La-Archanum aerodrome offered a wide array of interesting ship upgrades. Beyond the default ones listed in Laergard there were unique extras.

Advanced Laser Cartridge: Improve the ATKP of ship laser turrets (**15,000 Gold Coins**)

MagiCannon Balls (Poison-Gas): Cannons with Aeri-engravings that create an additional effect upon impact (**30,000 Gold Coins**)

Ghost-Plating: Allows ship to go invisible for two minutes while in the air (**150,000 Gold Coins**)

The new upgrades had me so excited, especially the Ghost-Plating, but it was out of our price range. Unless I went back and sold the Zeratha's Isle discovery, which I didn't want to do. I also liked the sound of the MagiCannon Balls but wish they came with a different debuff from poison; I was fine fighting the soldiers on board these ships but wanted to minimize the damage done to the crew. In the end, I spent 10,000 gold coins buying two new laser turrets for the quarter deck, meaning we now had a full shooting radius for our turrets. I also bought the advanced laser cartridges to improve the strength of our shots. With the upgrade shopping done, I divided the plunder and everyone got a massive payday. The crew morale jumped back to over-joyed, though I was sure it would be back in the negative by the next time we docked.

The errands were done. I hurried back through the market of floor-0 and down a spiraling staircase to floor-1.

The hallways became dirtier and the beggar population expanded.

Our meeting point was *The Old Engine Pub*. The team sat at the back. Shade had a full pint in front of him alongside two empty pints sitting like trophies at the table. Serena had a glass of red wine and Kari was drinking water. Jackson was still off doing his own errands.

"What's up guys," I said. "You get the big payday message."

"Hell yeah we did," said Shade, slamming his pint on the table, like he was cheering for a sports team. "That's why we're celebrating."

"Excellent," I said. "Glad spirits are high. Have you guys managed to find anything out about Arethkar?"

"Not much," said Serena. "Everyone we asked either ignored us or changed the subject."

Changed the subject. Like the assistant at the skyfarer's guild.

"There's something going on here," said Kari, holding her glass of water with both hands. "Something the citizens of this place aren't telling us."

"Because there's nothing to tell," spat a drunk man, next to our booth.

"What do you mean?"

"La-Archanum is an independent state. Neutral to all the bullshit of you groundlings."

"It must be nice to not be involved in such politics," I said.

The drunk man looked away and said melancholically, "Bah! There'll come a time in this great war when everyone will be forced to pick a side."

The man's eyes rolled back and his jaw slacked, drool falling out as he snored away into sudden unconsciousness.

"What the heck does that mean?" said Serena.

"Beats me," I said. "I'm getting a drink."

I stepped towards the bar and the pub's door swung open. A trio of red bandana guards stepped into the bar, scabbards and pistols pointed at us. One of them growled at Shade. "Did you really believe someone as infamous as yourself could waltz into La-Archanum and go unnoticed?"

"I have no idea what you're talking about," said Shade.

"Save it," spat the guard and then turned to me. "Captain Clay Hopewell of the *Horizon's Dream*—you and your party are under arrest. The Grand Captain Bella would like to see you."

One of the guards behind Bella spoke up. "Sorry man, but we're not really into alliances. Governments in general."

Sorry man? The three guards behind Bella were members of The Chosen.

"Wait—you guys are players?"

Bella smirked and kept her eyes on Shade. "You're not the only one who befriended The Chosen, Shade. They are quite practical and useful I've found."

I ignored Bella and looked at the guards. "Guys—I hate to interrupt whatever reverse harem pirate roleplay sesh you guys got going on here *but* we need your help. It's in your interest to help us. Arethkar is enslaving its players."

The first guard replied to my plea. "Every single government on Earth said those very lines: *it's in your interest to buy into our system.* Yet what did the government do for us out here, huh? What did they do as the ZERO virus ravaged through it all? Nothing. Now you want us to make peace with these groundlings, forget it."

Barter (Level 2) Failed
You increased your bartering skills by 0.1

Damn. Their guns remained raised. They weren't interested in an alliance. What else did we have to bargain with? I had an idea.

"Okay, I get it," I said. "You're not interested in peace with us. How about a compromise?"

"You want an alliance, we don't," said Bella. "I don't see else there is to say?"

"You don't want an alliance," I said. "But there's something else you want. Untold riches, perhaps. What if I told knew the location of Zeratha's Isle?"

21

The red bandana pirates led us through the ringed streets of La-Archanum towards a grand elevator. It was tall and made of gold and went up through the ceiling towards the other floors. Another set of guards walked behind us, swords unsheathed.

The elevator chimed and the doors slid open. We all stepped in. Us and our armed escorts. We were silent. At least, ostensibly.

Serena: Shade—you said you were on good terms with these people?
Shade: When I said good terms, I actually meant bad terms.
Kari: Pretty big mistake Shade.
Shade: Don't hate the player, hate the game!
Serena: How do I do the eye roll emoji?
Clay: Guys, we need to think this through. Shade—how bad terms are you with this Grand Captain Bella? Is there any chance we can salvage an alliance with her and her city?

Shade: Let's just say, she's a bit intense.
Serena: What does that even mean? "Intense"?
Shade: She actually reminds me of you S.

A light flashed at the top as we passed through each floor: Floor-0, Floor+1, Floor+2, and finally stopping at the top, Floor+3. The door slid open and we stepped out into an airy penthouse suite. Starlight fell through the clear glass of the atrium overhead. Three pirate Lirana stood in the middle of the room. One wore a red bandana like the other pirates we'd seen, another wore a more conventional pirate jacket, and the third had a gold tooth smile. They kept guard around a chaise longue with a Lirana woman lounging comfortably on it, legs stretched out with glossy black-heeled boots at the end of them. Her tanned legs were bare. The only clothing she wore was a lacy one-piece corset, squishing her breasts together and concealing very little. She wore a pirate hat with poked out holes for her cat ears. She had one big green eye and another covered with a black eye patch. She had a long sword sheathed on either side of her with accompanying muskets. She had a white tail that twirled right above her tight ass.

This must be the pirate queen, Grand Captain Bella.

Kari: Serena—is it just me or has half our party gone brain dead?
Serena: The blood has clearly rushed to somewhere else ;)

Any attraction I had for the white-haired Lirana ended as she jumped to her feet and unsheathed her flintlock pistol and pointed it at Shade. The guards behind her all lifted up their guns to each of us.

"You got quite the balls showing up here," said Bella.
Shade lifted his hands to the side, signaling he came peace. "I don't understand the hostility Bella."
The pirate queen laughed and shook her head. "I you forgotten Shade? I haven't."
"Does anyone want to explain what's going on?" Serena. "Catch us up on whatever you're talking abou'
"Many moons ago, your pal Shade here talked flying away from Laergard and forming a new hom' Ariellum. Remember: that's what you called it? Th last minute, before we all departed into the together in spirit and ambition, he turned awa hope and gave up the cause. So why are you h' Don't you have another bottle to stare down?"
"Bella," said the Lirana thief. "There will nev Ariellum because Ariellum is gone, lost long no nation of Lirana to form it. Our world has have our people."
Bella looked Shade directly in the eye. Sh but she sure made it count. She then asses long stare. "You always had a soft spot for t I'm not surprised you've become friends Chosen, no less."
"We didn't come to open old wounds passing through on a quest for the King actually hoping to make you a propo between us and La-Archanum."
"Sorry love," said the pirate quee really our thing."

Barter (Level 2) Failed
You increased your bartering skills

The pirate queen's eyes widened. She gestured with her hands to the others to lower their weapons. The queen sat down on the couch. "Sit," she said, gesturing to nearby sofa chairs. "Talk to me."

Barter (Level 2) Success
You increased your bartering skills by 0.3
You've leveled up Bartering (Passive Skill) to Level 3!

We all looked to each other and sat down.

"Tell me more about the alliance you seek," said the pirate queen. "You see, La-Archanum has survived many moons due to its neutral status in Illyrian affairs and so long as we service everyone here with our gambling, drinking, and other wares, it's fine. La-Archanum is more trouble than its worth. To keep it afloat. To stop near daily uprisings. Pirates are a tough bunch to rule over and the skies get more dangerous and difficult to navigate when there are warships passing across the clouds."

As Bella spoke, one guard walked around the room and pressed a button at the elevator. I messaged the others in party chat.

Clay: Guys, I think we're being trapped in here. Something's not right.

"All of which is to say," said Bella. "We're not against an alliance so long as it benefits us. However, when we gamble, we wanna bet on the winners."

"What are you saying?" said Shade.

An alarm went off and bars fell down on the windows.

Bella stood back up again, her pistol raised in one hand

and her sword gripped in another. There would be no talking her down this time.

"Sorry Shade," said the pirate Lirana queen, unsheathing her sword yet again. "But you guys are a sinking ship and I'm in the business of staying afloat."

In a quick flash, the three pirates were in front of their queen, cutlasses raised. A gust of wind blew my hair back as Serena back flipped over us and landed at the front of our group. "Protect Thy Allies!" she bellowed, sending a shockwave across the floor. The pirates all turned to her. They lunged forward, swords pointed at her heart. A sharp ring of steel against steel echoed through the room. Serena held up her blade in sword shield, blocking their incoming attacks.

Kari wasted no time, raising her staff, summoning a ball of golden white light into her small fox hands. She shot the beam out to Serena, the protective magic creating a bright aura around the warrior as it seeped into her skin.

The pirates pulled their cutlasses back and changed formation. The two at the sides moved to Serena's rear, overtaking her block radius. I stretched my arm and let out a torrential gust of wind from my palm. The air blast walloped the gold-toothed pirate, knocking him over.

The two other fighters slashed again at Serena. The blade soldier blocked their blows with her sword. *Damn, these guys were quick.* This was the first time we'd fought against other players. I'd always been more of a PvE guy over PvP. We needed to stay focused. These guys would think like gamers and the first thing they'd want to do is disorient us and use crowd control abilities. Status effects were king in PvP. A well-executed ability-cancel had the power to end a match in seconds.

I waved my hand through the air, directing my energy at the floor behind the pirates, coating it over with a freezing—

and most important, *slippery*—plate of ice. I then arched my elbows back, preparing to put all my strength into my next spell. I launched my arms forward, unleashing air blast, sending a propulsive gust of wind at the incoming pirates. Their bodies tumbled, tripped, and flew onto the hard floor of ice. Their health bars diminished while chilled and crippled debuffs flickered underneath.

I turned around, searching for an escape.

Across the room Shade and Bella traded knife blows. With each slash and block, a sharp clank echoed forth. The two Lirana circled each other.

"You talk about disloyalty Bella," hissed Shade. "What the hell is this?"

"I'm protecting my home."

Their daggers clinked and clanged as they knocked into each other. The two fighters barred their teeth and hissed at one another.

My eyes circled back to the pirates on the ice. They'd regained their composure, helping each other up. They each lifted their cutlasses into the air and clinked them together in a Three Musketeers, "All-for-one" kind of way. A wave of energy emanated from them and passed through me. What kind of team combo move had they initiated? I checked my HUD and saw it had picked it up.

Edward, Al, and Fisk initiate Parley

What the hell is parley!?

"Enough of this stalling," yelled Serena, rushing towards them, sword raised. She leaped in the air, preparing a crushing blow on the pirates. Yet something strange happened. As Serena flew through the air, her sword remained clutched behind her. It was in a prime position to swing, to arc across the air and land in the skull of one of the pirates, but she didn't move it. Serena landed on the ground, her attack stalled.

"What the heck is happening?"

I stretched my arm out. My arm made the motions of a fireblast, but no elemental magic exited my palm. My arm was like a gun with a jammed trigger.

Bad news: I was unable to attack.

Good news: whatever was effecting us was also happening to our opponents. They weren't even attempting to attack us. A message popped up in my HUD.

Parley (debuff): Offensive abilities disabled within the proximity of those with the pirate class. You're being attacked by pirates currently, you say? Arr shucks (duration: 3 minutes).

"What kind of weird move is this?" complained Kari.

"A bullshit one," said Shade, locked in a deadly staring match with Bella since they were unable to swing their blades at each other.

"I don't get it though," I said. "What's the point of negating all offensive abilities of your opponents, if it does the same thing to you?"

The red bandana pirate smirked. He clutched his fist and threw a coin in the air. A purple mist showering him as he did so. The two other pirates followed suit, even Bella did something similar.

Now what were they doing? My HUD laid it out for me.

Ed initiates Pirate's Philosophy
Al initiates Pirate's Philosophy
Fisk initiates Pirate's Philosophy
Bella initiates Pirate's Philosophy

"Here it comes guys," said Shade, taking another step back away from Bella. "Some extremely overpowered bullshit."

"What the heck is Pirate's Philosophy," said Kari, looking at our enemies with concern.

"It's an ethos," said Ed, clutching his sword with a new vigor and making practice swings in the air. "A way of life. A religion. A governing spirit. A set of rules"

"Basically, what he's trying to say," said Shade, frustration leaking into his voice. "Is pirates only follow one rule: *there are no rules.*"

"Exactly," said Bella, charging Shade with her cutlass.

The others headed towards us, swords raised.

"But what about the parley?" I said, taken aback by the onrush.

"Pirate's Philosophy stripped us of all our debuffs, bitch," yelled Ed, swiping his blade across the air in an attempt to slice Serena's head off. She met his attack with her blade raised. The metal clamored against each other, creating an awful shrill echo.

"Looks like we can still defend ourselves," said Serena between gritted teeth. She held her sword up against the onrush of attacks. "Kari—I need you to increase my Toughness stats and keep me healed."

"On it," said Kari, waving her staff in one hand and conjuring support magic in the other.

One of the pirates ran towards Kari.

"Aw hell no," yelled Serena. "Protect Thy Allies!"

A rippling wave shook through the room. The pirates gunning for Kari spun around with an urge to fight Serena.

"What are we supposed to do here if we can't attack?" I asked.

Serena triggered sword shield again. "Goddamnit! This would be so much easier if I could kick their teeth in."

"Do we have any updates on how we're supposed to get out of here?" I asked.

Kari stepped back and placed her hand on the elevator door button. She jammed her fingers into it repeatedly. No dice.

"The elevator's locked," said Kari. "There's a master key lock under here. If we can get the key, we can get out of here."

Shade stumbled backwards across the chamber, defending himself from Bella's onslaught of attacks.

"Too bad I hold the key," grinned Bella, lunging forward with her cutlass against Shade.

I checked the debuff timer on parley and saw we only had ten more seconds left.

"We'll be able to attack again in a few seconds guys," I said, revving myself up.

The pirates attacking Serena retreated and raised their cutlasses in the air again.

"Oh no," I yelled. "They're initiating parley again."

Serena ran towards them but without being able to attack, I didn't know how she'd be able to stop them. We needed to cancel the move without actually attacking them.

Aha.

I trigged electric blink, disappearing in a sparkle of electricity from the spot I was standing in, and reappearing on top of one of the pirates. I fell to the ground, collapsing on the cloaked pirate and dragged him to the floor with me, disrupting the trio from triggering parley.

I rolled over the pirate and got back to my feet.

"You shouldn't have been able to attack us," said Ed, red in the face.

"It wasn't an attack," I said. "I was simply falling with style. I call it coordinated buffoonery, dickhead."

"You're wasting your time."

I shook my head. "Serena, Kari—let's finish this," I yelled as I disappeared in a burst of electricity.

I reappeared behind Ed and threw out my hand, bright purple tendrils of electricity swirling around each of my fingers as I planted it into my enemy's head, offering free electric shock therapy. His whole body vibrated and shivered, seizing up and losing control of his senses.

Serena stomped the ground with her boots, triggering her move, *Release Me.* The two other pirates stumbled away from her. She took the clear path to Edward who had collapsed to his knees after my devastating attack. She leapt through the air, arching her giant sword behind her. As she came in for landing, Serena's blade touched the ground first, slicing through Edward's head and body, blood and guts flying everywhere. The two sides of his body bent and peeled in opposite direction like an unzipped jacket.

+148 EXP!

Serena hyperventilated. She lifted her blade from his divided corpse and turned to the next two players. *Right.* Our fight here wasn't over yet.

The two remaining pirates took a frightened step back as Serena turned towards them with her bloodstained sword. Their arms shook, their teeth chattered. They shared a nervous glance to one another. I suspected the parley and pirate's philosophy combo didn't work with only two.

The pirates gave a loud battle cry, regaining their lost confidence. They took a step towards us. I held my arm out and stretched my fingers wide, creating a small wave of fire at their feet. The flames got larger and larger until they curtained us from our attackers.

"Unleash the combo Serena," I said.

Kari waved her hands through the air, adding attack buffs to Serena. "Finish them!"

Serena ran towards the flame. She triggered blade tornado, becoming a swirling cyclone of unrelenting steel. She was a human chainsaw. The flame caught hold of her sword, enveloping it, and sharing its power with the blade. The pirates held up their cutlasses to stop the attack, but Serena's flaming great sword spinning at rapid speeds, simply knocked the thin swords out of the pirates' hands. Then, on the next rotation, it sliced through their bodies, cutting them in half, turning their corpses transparent even as she still spun.

+148 EXP!
+148 EXP!

"That was so badass," said Kari, turning to me. "Do you ever wish you were a tank?"

Serena, her arms covered in blood, shivered from the weight of the huge sword she held and fought with. I shook my head. It took a certain kind of strength to face one's fears as up close as she did.

"Guys," said Shade. "A little help... Please..."

Bella knelt overtop of Shade. His body was filled with

little cuts. Slits leaking blood and draining Shade of life. He only had a sliver of HP left.

"I don't want to do this," cried Bella, holding her knife with both hands over Shade's chest. "You know I hate to do this."

Bella was about to stab him. I turned to Kari, hoping to see a wave of healing magic shoot out of her hands, but instead she'd materialized an MP potion and was uncorking it to replenish her mana pool. We didn't have seconds to waste.

I lifted my chest and let a vapor of healing mist surround my person. I then pulled my hand back so it was aligned with my chest, surrounded by the curative mist. I pushed my hand out, triggering air blast. A gust of wind swirled out of my hand, capturing the particles of the healing mist in its movement. The airborne healing magic flew towards Shade as Bella's sharp knife descended towards his chest. My wind magic swept the healing particles onto Shade's skin, raising his HP by 30%. Cuts and wounds closed up and life returned to his face. My wind magic went an extra step further and knocked Bella over.

Shade scurried away from the close death. Kari flung out cure spells at him until he was back to max HP.

We stepped towards Bella who remained on the floor.

"Shade—she has the key to get off this floor and back to the ship. If we get going now, we can escape the Arethkarians coming to stop us. What do you wanna do?"

The pirate captain was on the ground, defenseless. Her life was currently in our hands. I didn't want to kill her. I understood her actions. Even if Shade disagreed, it was as Bella had said: *it was nothing personal.*

"Give us the key, Bella," said Shade, softly. "Give it to us and we'll go."

The captain grimaced, materializing the key in her hand. Shade swiped it out of her palm.

"You can't escape," said Bella. "Kaige and his crew docked while we were speaking. He won't let you leave."

"We'll see about that," said Shade. He turned around and left the pirate queen on the floor. He headed towards the elevator. It had been a brief trip, but our visit to La-Archanum was officially over.

22

Glass cracked. Broken shards rained down to the floor. We all looked up and saw the *Horizon's Dream* floating in the sky. Jackson poked his head over the edge of the deck. "Arethkarian ships have surrounded the city. We need to get out of here."

He tossed down a rope into the destroyed penthouse chamber.

"Shade you go first," I said. I wanted him to get away from Bella. I cast lightning cage and paralyzed her with the electric vines. She didn't fight it. Not one squirm. She'd given up. She wasn't evil this woman; all she had been doing was helping her people. Like I was doing. Like even Oren Kaige was doing. It made the pirate queen admirable, but also blind and dangerous as well.

Shade pulled himself up the rope, while Jackson threw down three more. I gripped the rope and pulled myself upwards. The door to the penthouse shook as somebody pounded behind it. I tightened my grip on the rope and pulled myself another few inches. The pounding didn't stop. It became the rhythm to my rope pulling until the pounding stopped with the metallic shriek of the elevator door wrenching open.

Oren Kaige stepped into the room. His boots crushed the shards of glass into dirt. He pointed his one remaining human hand at me.

"Your bold claims to take over Illyria end now," he said.

I hung halfway between the ceiling and floor. I turned around and pulled on the rope harder. Kaige's footsteps quickened as he ran across the room and leapt towards me. His pincer arm sliced across my legs, taking out a whopping 25% of my HP.

"Agh," I yelled. A hot burning pain embroiled my leg. I strengthened my grip on the rope. I didn't want to fall back to the penthouse where Kaige and his pincer arm waited. Thankfully, the rope was moving on its own. Crazy Jackson was dragging us through the clouds.

I clutched onto the rope and emerged from the skylight. I was now out in the open air.

"You won't always get away," bellowed Oren Kaige from below my feet.

I closed my eyes and took a deep breath. I hauled myself up another meter, getting closer to the deck. Shade was already up top and was helping Kari over the edge. Serena was ahead of me as well.

The wind whipped my hair. My nostrils filled with rushing air and the smell of burning mana exhaust. My palms and fingers ached. In the distance were the silhouettes of a fleet of ships. Metal slabs of destruction. Arethkarian warships. My stomach lurched. We were ahead of them in the quest for Ariellum, but barely. A lead they were clearly catching up on and fast.

Serena groaned as she pulled herself up the final bit, the others reaching and pulling her aboard.

I was slowing us all down the longer I stayed on this rope.

I kept my concentration and pulled. I released my legs from the rope and raised my chest to my gripped hands. I let go of one hand and reached higher up on the rope. I pulled my other hand up and then the rest of my body. I repeated this a few more times, slowly getting more and more nauseous, tired and sick. I pulled myself up and felt the warmth of other hands grabbing hold of my arm, then their strength as I was pulled up onto the deck.

I collapsed onto the wood and rolled on my back, hyperventilating.

"Just another day in the life of a sky captain," said Jackson offering me his hand. "Get used to it kid."

23

I stood up and took in the night sky around me. It didn't feel like a sea of clouds but rather an ocean of stars. The crew worked diligently on the sails.

"Emergency meeting," I said to the party. "Captain's quarters now."

The party came with me while the crew continued to work on keeping the ship moving forward, quickly and efficiently.

Once in my quarters, I materialized the map to Ariellum and laid it out on my desk. I straightened it and smoothed the crinkles of the old worn away parchment. I placed my finger on a faded dot on the map.

"We're more than halfway to Ariellum," I declared. The label was innocuous enough, but the surrounding areas on the map were more disconcerting. According to the old crumbling scroll, we were currently heading straight into a nest of deadly Sky Wyrms. My whole body shuddered at the thought. We'd encountered such creatures once before when we first travelled to Land's Shield. They were giant high-level sky serpents with dragon-like heads with teeth large and sharp enough to rip through airships. Without a doubt, we were nixing such a path to the gates of the fallen city.

To the west and east of the Sky Wyrms was a lightning belt wrapped around the area. Getting to the gates of Ariellum would be no easy feat. Everyone's skin was pale, goose bumps forming on their arms as they took in the difficult truth of our current situation.

"On top of the environmental obstacles facing us," I said. "Oren Kaige is on our heels."

The presence of the distant ships permeated through the room. "Will they be able to catch up with us?"

Jackson crossed his thick arms and harrumphed: sucking in air through his big nose and blowing it out in contemplation. "The Arethkarian ships are built with powerful engines. They also have a higher supply of mana fuel than we do; meaning, they won't depend on the wind as much as we will. They'll burn it all until they close in on us."

"Of course they'll close in on us," said Serena, pointing to the map in front of us. "We have nowhere forward where we can go."

"I say we hedge our bets and go through the lightning," said Shade. "It will give us a speed boost against the other ships."

Jackson shook his head. "The lightning belt is suicide."

"And the Sky Wyrms, aren't?" asked Kari.

The party turned to me. What was the most appealing: death in a lightning storm, prisoners onboard the Arethkarian armada, or the main course for Sky Wyrm dinner? Then I had an idea. A smirk grew on my face.

"I don't like that smile," said Serena.

"Neither do I," said Kari.

"What are you two talking about?" grinned Shade.

"That's the smile of a *plan*. An audacious, insane, they'll-never-be-able-to-pull-it-off plan."

"You say that like it's a good thing," said Kari, nudging the thief's leg with her elbow.

Shade's pointy cat ears wiggled. "I'm all ears, captain."

Jackson kept his arms crossed and grunted in accordance with Shade.

"Alright, listen up," I said, telling them the plan.

~

WIND WHIPPED ACROSS THE DECK. In the distance was the nest of Sky Wyrms. Their tails swayed through the clouds. We were too far away to make out any of their deadly heads, yet the hisses of their long tongues travelled through the air. My stomach lurched. The fleet of Arethkarian ships were getting closer and closer to us.

"As your first mate, I want you to know I think this plan is nuts," said Serena.

"I agree," said Shade. "Which is precisely why it's brilliant."

Jackson pulled the engine to a stop. The ship kept moving due to the wind but we weren't thrusting at the exact same speed anymore.

"I hope this works," said Serena, nervously.

I scratched the back of my head. "Congratulate me when we make it through."

"Oh I'll do more than that, hot stuff," she said and blew me a kiss. "If not, I'll make sure I kill you on our long flight to the bottom of this dismal sky."

The Arethkarian ships grew bigger as they approached.

Our ship rocked in the air of the starry night sky. Our

deck trembled as our enemy's ships approached us. We slowly drifted closer to the nest of Sky Wyrms.

"Let me know when," said Jackson.

The Arethkarian fleet was getting close. Their cannons and turrets were raised and locked onto our ship. We were seconds from being captured. Seconds from being destroyed. My leg shook, my foot shivering against the deck panel. A beam of light formed in one of the enemy turrets. It was now or never.

"NOW!" I yelled.

Jackson pulled back the engine lever, igniting the mana exhaust and shooting us forward towards the Sky Wyrms.

The ship flung through the air. Laser blasts followed us through the sky. The crew worked the masts, adjusting them to maneuver in and out of the incoming wave of attacks. The blasts hurled past us and towards the den of Sky Wyrms. The big red eyes of the monsters twitched and their mouths roared. The group of resting sky serpents untangled themselves and chased straight for us.

"Duck," I yelled.

Jackson maneuvered us below the incoming attack of Sky Wyrms as the creatures swirled through the air towards the Arethkarian fleet.

"Go, go, go," I said.

Jackson pulled the engine lever to the max, burning crystal mana fuel, shooting us through the sky. I held onto the deck as my hair flew back in the sky.

The Arethkarian fleet's attention turned to the Sky Wyrms attacking them. They wouldn't be catching up with us now.

I turned ahead and found we were in a new part of the cloud ocean. We were in a clear valley of stars. In the distance was the ring of lightning patches the map had described. We were nearing the gates of Ariellum.

In the middle of the star valley there was a golden doorway floating in the air. We approached it. I hoped the door would open as we got close. It didn't.

Shade pulled out his pistol and fired at it.

"What are you doing?" Serena yelled.

The bullet bounced off the door.

"Worth a try," the Lirana shrugged.

I rubbed my chin. I materialized the note Theobold had given me. He had written down the codes necessary for the quest, including opening the gates. Written on the scrap of paper was the necessary spell.

Run://open_dlc_content

I pulled my gloves off. To cast the spell correctly I needed my wrist bare. I pressed down on the swirling dark mass of the Prophetic Seal and cast the spell.

A beam of black energy shot out from my hand towards the golden gate.

The gates opened wide, emitting a bright light. A powerful force sucked us through the gate, teleporting us away from warring skies full of enemy ships and dangerous Sky Wyrms.

The red bandana pirates led us through the ringed streets of La-Archanum towards a grand elevator. It was tall and made of gold and went up through the ceiling towards the other floors. Another set of guards walked behind us, swords unsheathed.

The elevator chimed and the doors slid open. We all stepped in. Us and our armed escorts. We were silent. At least, ostensibly.

> **Serena:** Shade—you said you were on good terms with these people?
> **Shade:** When I said good terms, I actually meant bad terms.
> **Kari:** Pretty big mistake Shade.
> **Shade:** Don't hate the player, hate the game!
> **Serena:** How do I do the eye roll emoji?
> **Clay:** Guys, we need to think this through. Shade— how bad terms are you with this Grand Captain Bella? Is there any chance we can salvage an alliance with her and her city?

Shade: Let's just say, she's a bit intense.
Serena: What does that even mean? "Intense"?
Shade: She actually reminds me of you S.

A light flashed at the top as we passed through each floor: Floor-0, Floor+1, Floor+2, and finally stopping at the top, Floor+3. The door slid open and we stepped out into an airy penthouse suite. Starlight fell through the clear glass of the atrium overhead. Three pirate Lirana stood in the middle of the room. One wore a red bandana like the other pirates we'd seen, another wore a more conventional pirate jacket, and the third had a gold tooth smile. They kept guard around a chaise longue with a Lirana woman lounging comfortably on it, legs stretched out with glossy black-heeled boots at the end of them. Her tanned legs were bare. The only clothing she wore was a lacy one-piece corset, squishing her breasts together and concealing very little. She wore a pirate hat with poked out holes for her cat ears. She had one big green eye and another covered with a black eye patch. She had a long sword sheathed on either side of her with accompanying muskets. She had a white tail that twirled right above her tight ass.

This must be the pirate queen, Grand Captain Bella.

Kari: Serena—is it just me or has half our party gone brain dead?
Serena: The blood has clearly rushed to somewhere else ;)

Any attraction I had for the white-haired Lirana ended as she jumped to her feet and unsheathed her flintlock pistol and pointed it at Shade. The guards behind her all lifted up their guns to each of us.

"You got quite the balls showing up here," said Bella.

Shade lifted his hands to the side, signaling he came in peace. "I don't understand the hostility Bella."

The pirate queen laughed and shook her head. "Have you forgotten Shade? I haven't."

"Does anyone want to explain what's going on?" asked Serena. "Catch us up on whatever you're talking about."

"Many moons ago, your pal Shade here talked us into flying away from Laergard and forming a new home, a New Ariellum. Remember: that's what you called it? Then at the last minute, before we all departed into the unknown, together in spirit and ambition, he turned away. He lost hope and gave up the cause. So why are you here Shade? Don't you have another bottle to stare down?"

"Bella," said the Lirana thief. "There will never be a New Ariellum because Ariellum is gone, lost long ago. There is no nation of Lirana to form it. Our world has changed. So have our people."

Bella looked Shade directly in the eye. She only had one but she sure made it count. She then assessed me with a long stare. "You always had a soft spot for the groundlings. I'm not surprised you've become friends with a group of Chosen, no less."

"We didn't come to open old wounds," I said. "We are passing through on a quest for the King of Laergard. I was actually hoping to make you a proposition. An alliance between us and La-Archanum."

"Sorry love," said the pirate queen. "But allies aren't really our thing."

Barter (Level 2) Failed
You increased your bartering skills by 0.1

One of the guards behind Bella spoke up. "Sorry man, but we're not really into alliances. Governments in general."

Sorry man? The three guards behind Bella were members of The Chosen.

"Wait—you guys are players?"

Bella smirked and kept her eyes on Shade. "You're not the only one who befriended The Chosen, Shade. They are quite practical and useful I've found."

I ignored Bella and looked at the guards. "Guys—I hate to interrupt whatever reverse harem pirate roleplay sesh you guys got going on here *but* we need your help. It's in your interest to help us. Arethkar is enslaving its players."

The first guard replied to my plea. "Every single government on Earth said those very lines: *it's in your interest to buy into our system.* Yet what did the government do for us out there, huh? What did they do as the ZERO virus ravaged through it all? Nothing. Now you want us to make peace with these groundlings, forget it."

Barter (Level 2) Failed
You increased your bartering skills by 0.1

Damn. Their guns remained raised. They weren't interested in an alliance. What else did we have to bargain with?

I had an idea.

"Okay, I get it," I said. "You're not interested in an alliance with us. How about a compromise?"

"You want an alliance, we don't," said Bella. "I don't see what else there is to say?"

"You don't want an alliance," I said. "But there's something else you want. Untold riches, perhaps. What if I told you we knew the location of Zeratha's Isle?"

"Clay," yelled Serena, pulling out her sword. "What are we going to do?"

The monsters were seconds away from passing through the portal and joining our company in the bottom world.

I lifted up my arm and pressed the Prophetic Seal on my wrist casting, *run://close_dlc_content.* Black energy shot out of my palm towards the swirling portal. The blast hit the magical opening and the purple rims of energy closed. I fell to my knees, gasping.

"Clay! Are you okay?" said Serena and Kari, running up to me.

The portal was gone. Only empty gray sky. No trace of the gates ever being there. I'd sealed off the entrance to this forbidden place from our enemies, but had I also stopped us from ever getting back?

25

Staring out into the endless desert of ash and destruction, the party fell into disarray. The ship's crew morale was edging to defiant. The whispering didn't stop. The crew's faces were pale and shifty, full of furtive glances. They didn't understand why I'd taken them to this horrible place and sealed off our only way to get out.

Serena and Shade argued on what to do next as stormy gray clouds swirled above us. Every direction led to either ruins or empty desert. Our fates weren't looking good. Was I as wrongheaded as Bella, the pirate queen, who in her efforts to save her own people only brought them closer to destruction?

"We need to go to Ariellum," I said. "That's why we're here. That's where the Ultriga Weapon will be. We shouldn't procrastinate on this. There's no time. Let's go."

With my words, the party nodded their heads. We left the ship moored in the sand with the crew to protect it. We lowered a plank and the five of us walked onto the black desert plains and headed in the direction of the city ruins.

The crumbling ancient metropolis was nothing but a mere shadowy specter, a silhouette in the distance.

We trudged across the desert in silence. Shade walked behind us all, dragging his feet. His eyes winced at our gloomy surroundings. His body grimaced. We were walking through the sands of history.

"What's the story behind the Ultriga Weapon anyway?" asked Kari.

Shade sighed, not turning around to address the question. After a moment, he spoke. "It was a powerful weapon designed before the great rift. It was an allied effort, designed by Aeri and Lirana minds to combat the growing magitech strength of the Rorn. They created a weapon so powerful it shot a beam right through the grand continent, piercing the crystal core and causing the great rift."

"Oh wow," I said. "I knew the Ultriga Weapon was powerful but I didn't realize it was *that* powerful."

"It's part of the reason people hate the Aeri so much; they're blamed for changing Illyria forever, separating homes, families and cultures. Ripping out an old world and ushering in a new."

"But people don't hate the Lirana in the same way," I said. "Yet, from what you're saying, they were equally culpable."

"True," sighed Shade, still not looking at any of us, marching towards the ruined city. "But the Aeri never lost a continent, a capital city, and a home. Sure some blamed the Lirana, but my people have suffered. The Aeri continue as it is in their forest cities. Snobbish. It pisses people off."

We carried on our way towards the ruins. It was a quiet march. Low murmurs and whistles of the wind drifted across the desert of ash. Secrets to ancient civilizations, bone struc-

tures of lost creatures, and immense treasure all laid beneath
this dark black sand. It was all but forgotten, except for the
brief touch of wind over the ground it was buried under.

The area was barren and desolate. How did it connect to
the rest of Illyria? This zone was DLC content, so was it
instanced? Were we in a personalized version of the bottom
world, a world continuously refreshed for every new trav-
eller who sought it out? I shook my head. Maybe it was originally intended to work in such a way, back when A.K.O. was
being designed simply as a game, immersive entertainment
to get lost in, a distraction from the real world. In this incar-
nation though there was only one Ariellum. Only one set of
ruins. It was the only way to explain why we saw the Sky
Wyrms and the Arethkarian ships heading towards our
portal. This area and the outer Illyria were connected.

We continued forward, lost in our thoughts. Kari read
over her stats and abilities, while also taking note of our
own. She was figuring out how to accommodate her abilities
to everyone's play style and how to properly support the
team. Serena did breathing exercises, blade soldier yoga to
quicken her senses and make her more alert to her body
and surroundings. Jackson marched with the intent of a
soldier, his broad shoulders jutting back and forth as he
moved along. His gait was serious, yet his eyes peered
around with furtive and shifty glances. He was no longer
enslaved to the fighting pits, but he was still uncomfortable
with his new found freedom. Something so naturally
human wasn't coming easy to him. Not anymore. Not after
what he'd been through.

Shade walked at the front of our party, trudging determinedly towards the ruins. What would we find there?
Would Shade be happy with anything we came across? We
were walking through the remains of a place his people

once called home. Was this what it would feel like for us to return to the real world?

My thoughts echoed back to me. This place. It was originally intended to be a distraction. A piece of entertainment. Something you did to forget your homework, your shitty job and crummy life and the unfairness of the world with its corrupt politicians and crooks. Who knew this "distraction" would end up becoming for so many of us a reality to rival our own? A place of refuge in a lost world. A distraction that became a home, a shelter in a storm.

The city was in closer view now. Fallen dilapidated columns and the crumbling remains of stone houses appeared in the distance.

The floor at our feet trembled. Mounds of sand kicked up and headed towards us. Something slithered through the blackened dirt.

"What's that?" asked Kari.

"We're not the only living things down here," I said.

"I don't know about living," said Jackson, punching his fists together and buffing himself for battle. "But there's definitely something here that wants to mess with us."

The creatures moved across the desert floor. I still had no idea what was fast approaching towards us, what creatures we were about to face. The last thing I had fought with the ability to burrow and traverse underground was Cuddles, the giant scorpion from the arena pits of the Grand Casino Palace. The very thought made my skin crawl. Were we about to fight *two* giant scorpions?

Serena held her sword out, hands gripped tightly around the handle.

Shade crouched with both of his daggers drawn, preparing to strike, dodge, and maneuver around this new enemy.

Jackson knocked his fists against his chest, stacking ATKP and TGH buffs.

Kari lifted her staff, sending protect magic onto Serena.

I let my arms hang at my sides, fingers twitching ready to cast whatever spell was necessary.

The mounds of dirt got closer and closer. "Here they come!"

Erupting from the ground and shooting high into the air was a [Sand Shark], followed by another. Twenty feet long, the scaly creature was silver-skinned and had purple eyes on its side. It floated in the air, flipping high above us and diving straight back beneath the ground we stood on. The creatures slid through the sand like fish in water.

Everybody tensed, eyes falling to the ground. I tracked the movement of our underground attackers.

"How are we supposed to fight these things?" yelled Serena, full of frustration. She jabbed her sword into the sand like she was playing whack-a-mole. "Come out and play."

One shark erupted from the ground, dealing an uppercut head jab, smashing its nose into Serena's chin. The blade soldier fell from the attack, taking a 35 HP hit.

"Serena!" yelled Kari, sending a blast of golden healing magic her way.

The knight stood up and wiped the blood from her mouth. "Hit these bastards with Earthquake, Clay. Show 'em what you can do to the ground they love so much."

"Gotcha," I said, stretching out my arms and directing my magic at the mounds of dirt circling us. The sand sucked in on itself. Hardened. Rippled with destruction. The sand sharks shot out of the damaged ground, escaping the clutches of my spell.

In the air, they met the fury of Jackson's roundhouse

karate kick. The Rorn brawler ricocheted off one silver fin and landed on the flesh of the other sand shark, detonating a powerful punch into the companion creature's nose. The monster squealed, falling back towards the black sand. Jackson fell with it, letting out a flurry of punches. He pushed the creature to the ground even faster than it was falling. The red HP bar above the creature dropped below 50%. Meanwhile, the shark Jackson had bounced off regained its composure, back flipping and diving into the depths of the black sand.

"Time for some Earth magic, homie," shouted Shade, eyeing up the ground with his daggers in hand.

"On it," I said, tracking the movement in the sand, the rippling black ash. Once I spotted the creature, I stretched out my arm and directed another earthquake spell at where it was heading. The ground hardened and cracked into sharp pieces of stone. The sand shark burst forth from the ground, jumping through the air towards me, teeth wide open and ready to chomp my head and swallow it whole.

Serena pounded her chest and shouted, "Protect Thy Allies!"

The sand shark pivoted in the air, heading towards Serena. She readied her blade in sword shield. The shark's teeth clanked against the steel of the blade. Serena gritted her teeth. Her face reddened as she battled with the sand shark.

"Serena—hold on!" Kari lifted both her hands, summoning a bright white orb. She volleyed the energy ball towards Serena. The silver healing magic flew through the air and bounced right on top of Serena's head, showering the spell and its defensive enhancements all over Serena's person.

The shark flipped in the air, dove quickly back into the

sand, only to erupt again, knocking Serena back. She quickly jumped back to her feet, sword at hand. "I can't keep waiting forever. Shade—where the hell are you?"

Emerging out of stealth, Shade dug his two daggers into the back of the sand shark. It cried out in pain and agony. Shade's backstab attack triggered a stack of critical hits.

The shark was now off balance, composure lost. Serena wasted no time. She charged straight up to the monster, leaping in the air with her sword high above her head. She arced the blade downward, falling to the ground with the killing blow. The sword sliced through the silver sand shark, two halves flopping over onto the sand, leaving a puddle of entrails and blood.

+133 EXP!

Jackson grunted and groaned. He was wrestling with the shark. He gripped both ends of its jaws and was twisting them apart. His muscles bulged and sweat rolled down his face as he tore the monster in two.

+133 EXP!

He dropped the dead shark to the ground. He let out a long sigh. He rubbed his hands and turned to us. "That shark seriously required all three of you to kill it?"

We all stared at Jackson dumbfounded and shrugged. We turned towards our destination.

The sand at our feet thinned, revealing old stone walkways of the ancient city. The endless mounds of ash made way for fallen stone columns and the remnants of old homes. Welcome to the lost city of Ariellum. Population: zero.

26

"What a ghost town," said Serena.

Shade and I ignored the ruins in front of us and went over to the fallen sand sharks, looting them for materials. We were on the clock, but these sand sharks were rare creatures.

Shade dug his knife into the creature's gums, loosening out a sharp angled tooth, until he held it between his grip. "Sand shark tooth—useful for shamanic and alchemic recipes. This will net us a pretty penny back at Land's Shield. Carve out as many as you can."

I pulled out my trusty basic sword and got to work, playing demented dentist on the dead sand sharks. Looting the creatures was methodical and satisfying work. First we gathered their teeth, then we carved off their carcasses into slabs of meat, then we collected their bones. It was a whole boatload of materials I was excited to play around with and craft later. I was also super pumped, because even though it was a ton of material, I didn't feel the weight of it at all, as it remained handily away in my inventory. I was looking forward to the shark burger I'd make and devour later.

With looting done, I returned to the conversation.

"It's amazing so much of the architecture has still survived," said Kari.

"They say Ariellum was a thriving metropolis back in its time," said Jackson. "A technological epicenter rivaling the great Rorn cave cities of old."

"And what is it now?" murmured Shade, cutting off our conversation. "Nothing but ruins and ash. What good did being the epicenter do it? What was so crucial about techno-logical advancement?"

"Didn't you say it had to do with wars with the Rorn and the Aeri?" said Serena.

"There's always war. Always politics. And there's always the poor chumps caught in the middle of it all. Victims of context, I'd say. The classic wrong place at the wrong time. That's what happens to—what was the phrase Kari?—the average Joe."

There was a lot of truth in what Shade was saying. Look where we were: potentially trapped in a desolate wasteland full of carnivorous sand sharks and what for? To control the flow of power between the rival nations of Illyria. I knew it wasn't so simple. We were fighting for a good cause: to save the average Joe being enslaved over in Arethkar, to stop them from coming to Laergard and inflicting the same forced labor on the rest of us. We had good reasons to fight, but Shade was right: we'd never asked for those reasons. They were thrust upon us.

"C'mon Shade," I said. "We gotta keep our heads up. We need to find the Ultriga Weapon and bring it back with us, so we can stop Arethkar and stop their madness. Save all the average Joes in peril of falling victim to poor circumstances."

Shade nodded his head, glumly.

"Plus," I added. "When this is all finished we'll have a

huge feast of sand shark burgers and mead for days. Did you hear that Shade? Mead for freaking days!"

"Aye," said Shade, cracking a grin, smiling at the thought of delicious beer. "You know just what to say to cheer me up."

The happy moment didn't last very long. Walking through the main thoroughfare of the ruins was a band of three warrior mobs, clad in ripped ragged clothing. Above their heads was the nameplate title: [Fallen Soldier]. They were kind of like zombies: gray emaciated skin, sickly bald heads, and lifeless eyes the color of pure white marble. That was where any comparison to classic undead monsters ended. Jutting out along their arms and out the back of their necks were an assortment of black obsidian spikes as well as the odd purple crystal, glowing across their gray skin.

"What are those?" asked Kari, clutching her healer's staff.

"The fallen," said Jackson. "Denizens of the bottom world. They can live centuries off very little sustenance, but when they find prey, they make sure to eat more than people's flesh, but their souls as well."

"What the heck does that mean?" said Serena. "Our souls!? Will we not respawn if killed by these things?"

"You'll respawn but you'll pay an additional penalty," said Jackson. "If the rumors are to be believed, the fallen are able to strip player's of their memories. Not a noticeable amount at first, but enough deaths from the fallen will leave you not knowing who you are or where you came from."

"Damn," I said. "Let's not screw around with these things then. Bring it on."

The fallen soldiers approached, waddling slowly towards us. Their mouths hung open like wolves excited at new found prey. Their teeth were rotten and brown. The decomposing figures were eager for flesh and memories to devour.

One stretched out its arms and opened its hands wide.

Kari cast defensive buffs, first on Serena, and then on the rest of us. The fallen soldier kept its arm stretched out, its palm open wide. It grimaced and shivered as a hole opened up in the center of the soldier's hand. Emerging from its gray flesh was a sharp piece of obsidian rock. It screamed and the sharp bones launched from the creature's hand and came flying towards us.

"Cover!"

We all ducked out of the way of the projectile.

"We got at least one ranged fighter to deal with then," I said. "Let's take it out first."

The two other fallen soldiers stretched out their arms. Black rock emerged from their palms. Uh-oh. Were they all going to be ranged? For one soldier, the black bone morphed into a spear, attached to its arm. The other bone seeped out of its palm and between its knuckles, creating bone claws on either hand.

I stretched out my arm and swept it from right to left in front of me, conjuring a flame wall to divide us and the fallen.

"Remember guys," I said. "Certain moves can combo with my flame walls. Don't hesitate to try."

Shade assented to this plan with the bursting sound of his flintlock pistols firing. The bullets zoomed across the ruined ancient pathway, gathering renewed burning energy as it passed through my walls of flames. The bullets smashed into the spear soldier, igniting his chest with fire. His HP took a hit along with a burning debuff draining him of even more health. He patted down the flames, the burning debuff flickering away.

"Oh baby," said Shade. "Can somebody say flame bullets!" He fired off more pistol rounds, shooting my conjured wall of flames.

Emerging from the other side was the sharp obsidian bone. As it passed through the fire, it too took on a fiery hue.

"Damn, they're using your own magic against you," said Serena.

"It's bullshit," I said. "New plan. Serena go take on the two melee fighters."

"I don't know if I can take all those hits," said Serena. "Even with Kari healing me."

"Well, Jackson and Shade are going to sneak around and take out the ranged soldier."

"They will take a few seconds while I'll be bombarded."

That's your job as tank, I wanted to say. Why was she hesitating? It was the threat to our memories. Serena was fighting with extra caution, fearing her memories. Everyone was.

"Understood," I said. "I'll blink and occupy the ranged monster while I wait for back-up. Sound good?"

"Sounds crazy," said Serena.

Serena made a war cry and ran towards the fallen creatures. She leapt in the air and triggered charge strike, her whole body shot through the upper portion of my flame wall, taking on a fiery hue. She transitioned into blade tornado, spinning in an intense circle of spinning metal like a flaming chainsaw. Her attack smashed into the two melee soldiers. They attempted to block the attack, but the cumulative power of her sprint, charge attack, and blade tornado knocked the two soldiers back. They were stunned and burned by her molten hot sword.

"Protect Thy Allies," yelled Serena, pulling in all the aggro and hate from the enemy mobs. The spear soldier came running at her. She kicked it at bay and turned around in time to clash blade against blade with the sword-armed fallen soldier. The monster threw out a left hook with its other bladed hand. Serena pulled her head back, barely dodging the deadly blow. She retaliated by head butting the creature in the face, knocking it back a step.

The ranged soldier stretched out its arm, powering up another bone blast, heading straight for Serena.

Time to move. Or rather, blink.

"You guys better be quick and come save my ass," I said to Shade and Jackson. I initiated electric blink.

I emerged in a sparkle of electricity in front of the ranged fallen soldier. The fallen triggered its projectile blast. I reached out my hand, fingers stretched out and crackling with electricity. I unleashed lightning cage, cancelling the fallen's ranged attack.

The monstrous fallen soldier shrieked and held up its hands, running towards me.

"Ick, get away," I said, triggering flame dodge, sliding away from the monster. I escaped with ease but it had unintended consequences. The fallen soldier turned its attention away from me and back at Serena.

"No, you dumb monster crud," I said, charging up a fireball in the palm of my hand and whipping it at the soldier. "Fight me!"

The molten ball of flame to the side of its head was enough to regain its attention.

"That's right," I said. "Come to me."

The fallen soldier dodged my second fireball. He emerged from his roll, arm cocked on his knee, and let out his own bone blast. The projectile moved swiftly through the air. It clipped my shoulder. A sharp pain pierced my upper body and knocked me back a step.

"Agh," I cried, reaching up to the wound and finding my fingers, covered in blood.

Two status warnings popped up in my HUD.

Bleeding (heavy) (debuff): *You have an open wound. You will lose 3 HP every ten seconds. You cannot regenerate health until you stop bleeding.*

Shock (debuff): *What's this? Blood? It's freaking you out. No shit, Sherlock. You're shocked! (Duration: 1 minute)*

My vision wobbled. I fell to my knees.

The fallen soldier returned his focus on Serena. He threw two more bone shards towards the blade soldier. There was no way to stop them.

Kari was dedicating all her focus on healing and protecting Serena. Those two bone shards coming in at the speed of a professional baseball pitcher would not help their cause.

I had to get the fallen soldier's attention back on me. I shut my eyes and triggered electric blink and when I opened them again, I was inches away from the awful creature's face. I lifted my arms to do skull shock, but it swatted my hands away and clasped me with its gray decrepit fingernails. It placed its dry rough hands onto my cheeks.

My whole body went very cold. It was a frostiness that sunk underneath your skin, bristled through your veins and wrapped its icy grip around your bones. I felt not just a physical coldness, but a mental and emotional one too. Like my mind was drowning in a frozen lake and the surface was icing over, sealing me out.

My HUD flashed.

Memory Drain (debuff): What's going on? Who am I? Why is there a status screen expressing my thoughts? Oh snap! You're losing your memory (duration: ∞)

I was struggling to breathe. Was it my memories disappearing or was my body forgetting how to function as well?

Then the coldness was gone. So was the battlefield. The pain. The urgency. Then nothing at all.

∽

I WAS IN A HOSPITAL ROOM, sitting on a visitor's chair. My brother was on a bed with wires and tubes attached to him. He had a broken arm. He had fought the group of kids who had wanted to steal my lunch money. I didn't understand: the trade-off wasn't worth it.

"Why didn't you let me give them my money?

He looked up to the ceiling stoically. His plastered arm forced to rest over his stomach.

"You're my younger brother, I wasn't going to let them disrespect you and our family."

"But was it worth getting sent to the hospital?"

"When you do something right for the sake of your family, to hell with the consequences!"

"Thanks big bro."

He kept his eyes to the ceiling of our bedroom, pissed off with the state of his broken body. "Anytime bro. Anytime—"

∽

"CLAY!"

Serena shook me awake. Where was I? What was happening? The battle with the fallen soldiers came back to me. The horrible decrepit hands reaching up to me. It stole my memories.

The three soldiers were now dead on the ground.

"They took my—" I raised my hands to my head.

"You're okay," said Jackson. "They will come back to you. They weren't permanently taken. They can only take when they kill you and fortunately, we were only a second or two away from pummeling him to death before he grabbed you. Why'd you electric blink so close to him?"

"I wanted to stop Serena from taking anymore damage," I said. My vision spun and my eyes struggled to stay open. I was lethargic, like I'd woken up from an afternoon nap and wasn't sure who I was or where I was going or what I was doing.

Serena grabbed my hand and smiled. "Thanks hon. They were powerful. I appreciate you taking some of the hits."

"Where did you go?" said Kari.

"I dunno. It was a memory of my brother and me as kids. It was weird."

"Freaky," said Kari.

"Let's keep moving," said Serena.

"Agreed," added Jackson, crossing his arms and glancing towards the ruined city.

"Well, if we're ready to go," said Shade, pointing up to the end of the thoroughfare we were currently on, specifically at a temple-looking structure at the top of the hill. "That's the temple of the ancients. Anything placed under protection would've been put there. It's where leaders were said to have been buried."

"Great—an ancient burial site," I grinned as I stood up. "What could possibly go wrong?"

27

Before we headed up towards the temple, we quickly looted the fallen soldiers. Yes, we were in a rush to get out of there, but these were unique mobs and the chances of encountering them elsewhere were slim. Any drops they left behind were bound to be valuable and rare.

This line of thinking proved to be true. The purple shards on their backs were called "mnemonic stones." They were what powered these creatures, gave them life but also the hunger for people's memories. The blackened shards were called "Obsidian Stones of Forgetting." There were more of them than the pink mnemonic stones. I had a feeling the mnemonic stones slowly turned into the "Obsidian Stones of Forgetting" after a certain period of time.

"But if this place is locked from the rest of Illyria, how have these things survived? What memories have they fed off?"

"From the memories of the dying Lirana of Ariellum," said Shade. He carved out a stone from the back of the fallen soldier and tugged at its body as he ripped it off.

We gathered all the drops and continued on our way. The crumbling remains of the temple loomed over the city. Half-standing columns and toppled corniced rooftops laid on the ground where a once glorious structure stood. Nothing grew amongst the ruined homes we passed. Not a vine or plant grew in the windows where I'm sure flowerpots used to hang. The remnants of drain pipes and canals only housed skeletons and dirt. The streets where young Lirana children once played were now dead and deserted. The same streets where men and women went to work. Merchants, politicians, technicians, historians. A whole culture of Lirana—similar yet vastly different from the one I'd come to know. A Lirana not burdened by guilt, loss, and melancholy for a world that no longer was. Such a peaceful thought still lingered here. I blinked and was brought back to the hollow crumbling ruins we were walking through. The peaceful thought was only that. A thought. An idle fancy. A daydream.

At the end of the thoroughfare was a winding stairwell leading up to the temple. The staircase wound around the hilltop.

We walked up the steps and arrived at the first platform. Waiting for us there were three more fallen soldiers.

"Give me a break," sighed Kari. "My MP just replenished back to full."

"Let's change up our tactics this time, yeah?" I said. "Serena—still draw their hate with your "Protect Thy Allies" ability, but once you've drawn their aggro, kite them. Shade and Jackson, you guys take them from the rear. I'll try and crowd control them with my spells. Everybody ready?"

"Ready!"

Serena ran into the center of the platform and beat her chest with her fist. "Protect Thy Allies!"

The fallen wailed and turned towards her. She charge striked away from them and they followed her.

My arms stretched out and my hands clawed at the air, manipulating the ground at the feet of the fallen soldiers. The dirt cracked and rippled, shards of stone stabbed them and tripped them over. The crippled debuff sign flickered underneath their status bars. Next I conjured two swirling balls of fire in each of my hands and blasted them off to the rippling ground. The combo sparked and the crackling ruptured ground turned molten with hot lava causing the creatures even more pain.

With all the AoE damage I was inflicting, I'd gained the enemies' aggro. They headed towards me. Their bone weapons emerging from their palms.

"Protect Thy Allies!" bellowed Serena again, retriggering their hate back onto her.

The monsters stumbled across the molten landscape I had created. Jackson leapt across my area of burning rock with a spinning kick, lodging it right into a fallen soldier's face. The creature's neck twisted. A cracking sound echoed across the battlefield. The fallen twisted its neck back to center.

Shade slid through the legs of one and emerged beneath another and unleashed mug shot with his daggers. It was basically a frontward facing backstab. The knife dug into the fallen's chest. Crimson blood spurted out from the hole his knife left.

Right as the creatures turned their sights on our melee DPS squad, Serena triggered her "Protect Thy Allies" move again. The creatures chased after her. Shade and Jackson subsequently retreated and I returned to crowd controlling them.

I stretched out my arms and opened up my palms and pushed. A gale of wind emerged and knocked the creatures back a step. I quickly swiped my arms across the battlefield and turned the once burning and broken rock into a sheet of ice. They clamored after Serena and even tripped onto the ice to do so. Their movement was now slowed to a crawl. This was our chance to finish them off. My hand crackled with lightning and I threw out a whip of electric energy. The lightning cage wrapped around one of the fallen, paralyzing him completely.

"It's all or nothing now guys!"

The group descended on the weakened fallen with Serena leading the charge. She charge striked her way to the center of them and unleashed blade tornado, slicing up their flesh and skin. Jackson dealt intense punches and blows to their stomach, shattering their black obsidian bones from the inside out. Amidst this chaos, Shade triggered backstab on the fallen soldiers with ease. They were too distracted to see a well-timed stealth attack in the midst of such a flurry of activity. Even Kari threw out her offensive magic—holy spells that dealt a considerable amount of damage.

The creatures fell to the ground and the experience points rushed across my HUD.

+147 EXP!
+147 EXP!
+147 EXP!

"Nice," I said, heading over to the bodies and materializing my sword. I carved out the mnemonic stones and obsidian shards from the dead mobs.

After I finished gathering all the materials, I stood up

straight and took in the stairs. Still a ways to go to get to the top. I stepped forward and the party followed after me.

We continued up the steps. Every platform had another set of three fallen soldiers. They got progressively tougher to beat the further we went up. Their special bone abilities got more and more unique. One of them created sharp prickles from all over his body, making it impossible to get close to him. Another's spinal cord stretched out from its neck and attacked like a scorpion pincer. The tough mobs meant we were close to the Ultriga Weapon.

We reached the summit of the winding steps, out of breath and exhausted.

"Tell me this is the end," huffed Kari. "I never realized what a pain it would be to be so small. For every step *you* take, I take three more!"

"Yes—but think of all the places you can hide," said Shade. "Plus, it's cute how small you are."

Kari's cheeks blushed. Then she went red in the face all over. "I was going to say thanks but then I remembered who I was talking too! What do you want Mr. Suave Persuasion, so many stats in luck he's basically cheated the system?"

Shade grinned. "I guess you saw right through me. I thought it might make you take the bad news more easily."

Kari's shoulders dropped. "What bad news?"

Shade stepped out of her way and presented the entrance to the temple. It was another stairwell. This time spiraling below the ground.

"You'd think they would put the entrance at the bottom then."

"Too easy," said Shade. "Shall we?"

28

The entrance to the crypt was a doorway of shadows. A few steps and then nothing but blackness. I conjured a fireball in my hands and lifted it up above my head.

"Clay Hopewell—human torch," smirked Serena. "Lead the way."

I took a step into the passage. A rustle echoed through the chamber. The staircase spiraled downwards. We continued deeper into the darkness. A faint glowing light emerged. It was coming from the bottom. I hurried my pace and everyone asked me to slow down. The human flashlight was moving too fast for everyone.

We got to the bottom and the light was glowing in a large square chamber across a hallway.

"The Ultriga Weapon might be in there," said Jackson. "But one thing is for certain. That's a boss room."

"Isn't there usually a glowy purple flame to indicate the final room of a dungeon?" said Serena.

"We're not in a dungeon," I said. "This is a temple, remember?"

"Temple, shmemple," muttered Kari. "Looks like a dungeon to me."

"Alright guys," I said. "This is the moment we've been waiting for. We're getting closer to the end of this quest. Follow my lead. Be ready for any traps or—despite it not being a dungeon and clearly a temple—a boss monster."

We hurried down the hall and entered the large chamber. In the center was a lectern. Resting above it on a stand was a silver turret attachment, similar to the guns attached to the *Horizon's Dream*. The end of the barrel had four pincer-like claws.

"Do you guys think that's it?" I said, taking a step closer to it.

I was still a good few meters away from the device when the room shook. The floor trembled. The walls vibrated. Rocks from the ceiling fell to the ground. A golden light formed in the center of the room, right beside the pedestal. The light slowly grew bigger, taking on the contours of a person. It was like a golden hologram. The shining body grew a tail and cat ears. It was a Lirana ghost. From a plain doll-like figure, the ghost grew a set of ethereal samurai armor and swords sheathed at its side. A nameplate appeared above its head: [Spirit Warden].

"Who summons me?" bellowed the ghost. "Who steps into this sacred yet vile temple? Turn back now. Begone. Whatever you seek, it isn't worth it."

I swallowed the lump in my throat and spoke back to the spirit warden. "We seek the Ultriga Weapon. Our homeland is in danger from an invasion. The weapon is our only hope to save everyone we hold dear."

The spirit warden stepped towards us. His face was emotionless; yet it was detailed. He had once been an ordinary Lirana man. He wasn't born the guardian of this lost temple. The ethereal golden material of which he was composed, still captured the lines beneath his eyes, the furrow of his eyebrows. He must have been middle-aged when the fall of Ariellum had happened, when the Ultriga Weapon had shot through the core of the Illyrian continent. He was a warrior in a previous life. A general, or a sergeant. High-ranking and skilled enough to be trusted with the eternal task of protecting the legendary weapon.

"You seek safety through destruction?"

"Is it not necessary?" I asked. "Here you are with swords, guarding this device. Surely, you'd use violence to stop more violence from being dealt by the wrong hands."

The spirit guardian paused. "You are less foolish than you appear. Yet you sound like my people before we destroyed ourselves and our homeland."

Serena placed her hand on my shoulder and leaned towards me and whispered in my ear. "Do you think it's telling the truth? Should we listen to it?"

"It's a test," I whispered. "By walking away from it, it will give us the weapon. Sort of like: those who do not seek it, will get it kind of thing."

"I do not trick you mortal," bellowed the golden spirit at the center of the room. He stood there, motionless. Calm. Stoic. "And you cannot trick me. I see it in you all, the desire to acquire this ancient weapon, this artifact my people regret having made, this relic who others wish was destroyed centuries ago."

I wasn't expecting this. A monster or a demon perhaps but not a ghost warning us to walk away.

"You shouldn't take this weapon. It isn't right. It's cursed. This is my final offer: go at once or face my wrath."

We didn't move.

The spirit unsheathed its sword. "Please don't make the same mistakes we did."

We still didn't move. We made no gesture to leave.

"So be it," said the spirit.

The spirit guardian flickered then disappeared.

He reemerged right behind Kari and dug his golden translucent samurai sword right through her stomach.

Kari's whole face went pale. Her eyes bulged. The samurai spirit ripped out his blade. Blood seeped in a circle where the spirit sword had been. The crimson liquid stained her outside armor. She was down to 10% HP.

Jackson and Serena charged the spirit guardian, creating a division between the boss and our healer. Shade slid across the ground, grabbing Kari who'd fallen to the floor. He materialized an HP potion in his hand, ripped off the cork and poured the liquid down her throat.

Life returned to her face. Her HP meter jumped back up. The hole in her chest sealed. It was insane how much pain and destruction this game dished out and how quickly it was undone with a cure spell or a small potion of red liquid. It helped balance out the insanity.

"I'm sorry," Kari croaked. "I let you guys down."

"You didn't," said Shade, helping her up.

"Guys, don't lose focus," I said. Healing our healer at the start of a grueling boss battle was a terrible way to begin a fight. It got us off on the wrong foot. Bad for morale and bad tactically. We were now all over the place. Playing catch up.

Jackson spiraled in the air, delivering a wind-based drop kick. The move clashed with the spirit guardian's golden blade. Muscled leg against spirit blade. The two met, shaking the ground beneath them. They both pulled away. Jackson back flipped and landed cleanly back on the ground.

Serena came in next, delivering crushing blow to the spirit guardian's backside, but the boss was quick. He spun around and met the blade with his sword.

The boss was too fast. I had to slow him down before he used the devastating teleport ability again. A crippling debuff or two would diminish the power of his surprise attacks.

"Make sure you're casting defensive buffs on yourself as well Kari," I said. "His teleport ability means he can completely disrupt and undo our party formation. We need to be prepared for it."

"Sure!" said Kari, lifting her small staff and free hand in the air and showering herself with golden protect magic. A small shield icon flickered beneath her status bars.

I stretched out my arm and threw out lightning cage. A blue whip of electricity flew out from my palm and across the battlefield. The spirit warden stabbed the ground with his sword, creating a great gust of energy. The torrent of wind knocked Jackson and Serena back. The gale then disabled my lightning spell; the crackling lightning puttered and disappeared.

I swiped my arm across the air and circled back, conjuring a plate of ice in front of me. I then shut my eyes, disappearing in a crackle of electricity. I reemerged in front of the spirit warden, between Jackson and Serena. I wasted no time, stretching out my arms and pushing with as much force as I had. A gale of wind emerged from my push and propelled the spirit guardian onto my sheet of ice.

He calmly marched back across it towards us. The move didn't work. He was invulnerable to normal debuff spells.

"I'm really not digging this," I said. "Anyone have any ideas."

Kari shot off a heal spell towards the warden. His barely diminished HP went back to full.

"My bad," said Kari. "I thought it might work the same as the undead."

"It was worth a try," I said.

"Do you give up yet?" asked the spirit. "As you can see: you won't be able to defeat me."

He walked back towards us. Serena re-engaged him in a battle of swords while Jackson and Shade threw out attacks at his rear. The spirit was so fast, he was able to meet them all.

"There must be a trick here," I said. "Some way to stop him."

"There isn't," said Serena, between heavy breaths and swinging her sword. "He's protecting one of the most powerful weapons in the game. It makes sense he'd be difficult to beat."

He was able to block everyone's moves. Was he super fast or was he simply predicting all of our strikes? He must have a weak spot. We attacked him from all sides: back, front, rear. There was only one place left to try.

I electric blinked back into the fray, but this time I emerged right between the spirit guardian's legs. Looking up at the guardian's crotch, I lifted my hands and conjured two massive fireballs and launched them into the Spirit Guardian.

The guardian jumped up and retreated. His HP bar dropped by around 5%. He shook his head. He stretched out his arm and pointed his sword at us. He then dipped the sword to the ground and tapped one of the square platforms on the floor. The stone floorboard flickered away, revealing a starry spacescape below.

"This feels like one of my hangover dreams," said Shade, reloading his flintlock pistols.

"What happens if we fall in there?" asked Kari, clutching her healing staff closely.

"I don't want to find out," said Serena.

"Let's be careful," I said. "We're in a sealed off area of the game world right now. Like the fallen soldiers, death might work differently if we fall through there. There's good news though: he's immune from all angled attacks except from beneath him."

"I got just the move you guys," said Serena, rushing towards the spirit warden. She ran towards him, leapt in the air, triggered charge attack right towards his feet. She rolled upon landing, crouching beneath him. She swung her sword upward, yelling, "Upward Slash!"

Her blade swing launched the spirit guardian into the air like a volley ball player passing a ball to their teammate.

"Weak from below," said Serena. "Well, now is your shot."

"Great stuff," yelled Shade, sliding his guns into his waist and switching to his daggers with speed and grace. He ran towards the falling spirit warden and leapt in the air to meet him halfway with his knives. "I'm sorry Lirana ghost. This plan wasn't my idea, but if you're gonna mess with my friends, well, then, I'm gonna mess with you!"

Shade unleashed mug shot into the spirit's thighs. The warden's HP bar dropped by 3% from the critical hit.

The spirit regained composure as he fell and landed gracefully with one hand on the ground and the other resting behind his back for balance.

"Same tactic again," yelled Serena, running forward to face the Spirit Warden head on.

"Enough is enough," said the spirit. He stabbed his sword in the ground and the gust of wind knocked Serena back. She stumbled, edging closer to the gap and the starscape below.

"Serena!" I yelled. I threw out my arm and stretched my fingers wide, unleashing an air blast. The gale of wind shot from my hands in Serena's direction. I ran towards her, chasing the blast of wind I'd sent her way. I hoped it would knock her to the side away from the ledge.

But it didn't get there in time.

Serena fell through the gap into the space area. I dove towards the edge of the opening, holding out my hand, ready to grab onto hers. Yet looking over the edge, she was gone. Nothing was there. Just the empty nebulous galactic space of nowheresville.

I waited for the fallen party member prompt in my HUD, but it didn't appear. The missing confirmation only made me feel worse. A party member death would suggest death operated normally in this unlocked zone. Nothing meant abnormality. Nothing meant Serena was gone for good. My last real connection to my life prior to A.K.O. Someone who knew me before this, before the ZERO virus, before it all.

I stared down into the empty cloud of space. Shit. This was my fault. I'd brought Serena here. I'd made the decision to take this quest. All I wanted was to protect her and our future life together and yet here I was, facing her ultimate demise.

"Clay—watch out," yelled Shade.

I glanced over my shoulder and saw the shadow of the spirit warden. He lifted up his foot in preparation to knock me into the gap to nowhere.

I shut my eyes, disappearing into a crackle of electricity,

right as his foot was about to smash into my back. I reappeared across the chamber, tears in my eyes.

This guy had killed Serena. He was killing us all. How were we supposed to stop him?

There was one solution staring in front of me, but I refused to accept it. The spirit warden had told us from the very beginning to walk away. Turn around. Give up on the Ultriga Weapon. Was it really possible to do so? After Serena had fallen through the cracks of space and time. How did we walk away now? No. We wouldn't walk away. We'd defeat this thing and get the Ultriga Weapon for Serena's sake.

"Guys," I said, materializing an MP potion in my hand. "Keep it distracted."

Jackson and Shade nodded, charging towards the Spirit Guardian. Kari quickly cast protection and offensive buffs on both of them.

I guzzled down the blue liquid, feeling the fresh liquid mana course through my body and seep into my veins and replenish my magical abilities.

Time for my new plan. I shut my eyes, envisioning where I wanted to emerge in my blink, right below the spirit. I dematerialized into a burst of electric flashes and reappeared beneath the spirit. This time, however, I wasn't only going to attack its weak spot. I raised my hands, a cool power rushing through my wrists. A burst of lightning shot from my palms and wrapped around the spirit warden's thigh. A paralysis symbol flickered beneath its status bar.

I stayed put on the ground, conjuring a field of ice behind the spirit. I directed my hands at the warden, who was squirming in the grip of my lightning cage spell, and unleashed an air blast. I knocked him back and he skidded against the plate of ice.

Jackson and Shade ran to unleash a flurry of attacks, but the boss stood up remarkably quickly. The status debuffs disappeared. He stabbed his sword into the ground and knocked Shade and Jackson back.

He unsheathed another spirit sword, so he was now dual-wielding. "Time is running out," spoke the warden. He then yelled, "Ronin's Odds."

He disappeared in a flash. A sharp pain coursed through me. The spirit sword poked out of my stomach. The room spun. The blade slowly disappeared from view as the spirit warden dragged it from my bleeding flesh. I turned around, my hands sparkling with lightning, ready to land a hail-Mary stun shot, yet my hand impacted nothing but air. The spirit warden was gone.

He was behind Jackson, dealing the same wound he had to me. In seconds, he was behind Kari, then Shade. He returned to where he was. We were all in the red final bits of our health points.

Ronin's Odds: a samurai ability to even the playing field when fighting against multiple foes.

"Heal yourself first Kari," yelled Shade. "We're all dead if we can't heal."

Kari nodded determinedly and cast a cure spell on herself.

I expected another onslaught of attacks but instead, he sheathed his swords.

I materialized an HP potion and guzzled it down. My stomach wound sealed up as my health points shot back up into the green. Would it be enough to save me from what-ever attack the spirit warden was now initiating?

A powerful orb emanated from the spirit warden, growing out of him and getting larger and larger. The whole room began to disintegrate, the floor at the boss' feet shattering away and opening up the galactic starry space Serena had fallen into.

He was self-destructing, emitting a final explosion to destroy the infiltrators of his sacred temple.

"I am of the opinion we need to get the hell out of here," said Jackson.

"I concur," shouted Shade. "Oh boy, do I concur!"

"The hallway and stairs are our only option," said Kari, pointing towards the hall. They frantically looked to me, waiting for me to make the call to retreat, the official decision to escape.

The golden orb was getting larger, enveloping more and more of the room, shattering the dungeon façade for the empty space and stars lying beneath it. We only had one option left: run. Yet what about Serena? Where had she gone when she fell though the space in the floor? If we left now, was that it? Were we leaving Serena behind forever?

The thought—that Serena was dead and gone—paralyzed me. I would never see her again. Never spend any more time with her. Never reminisce of a world lost to us ever again. I never thought there was more of my old life and world to lose but Serena had been one last lucky piece of it and now she was gone too.

"Clay!" yelled Jackson, snapping me out of my funk. He was beside me, gripping my arm and pulling it. "Duck!"

Jackson dragged me to the ground with him. A huge projectile blast flew overtop of us. I closed my eyes. The trembling stone floor clamored against my kneecaps. A huge crash echoed across the chamber. The hallway—our exit route—was now caved in.

The room was already half-disintegrated.

Shade scratched the back of his head. "So, uh, anybody got any other ideas?"

29

The destructive golden orb emanated from the spirit warden, getting closer and closer. We were seconds away from death, unsure if we'd even respawn. We ran back towards the rubble blocking the hallway. Any inch gained against the approaching destruction was another second of life added.

Jackson bent over and picked up a piece of smashed wall and threw it to the side. He then threw more. Shade picked up smaller rocks and frantically tossed them aside as well. Kari helped out too. First she buffed Shade and Jackson's overall strength. She then lifted up tiny rocks to make it quicker and easier for our musclemen to get at the larger ones.

"Step away everyone," I said. "I have an idea."

The group was confused but did as I said. I pulled my staff from behind my back and clenched my free hand, drawing upon all the mana floating through the temple, and created the biggest earthquake spell I'd ever cast before.

The floor rumbled beneath my feet. The caved in hallway of rubble shook and disintegrated into smaller pieces of rock, opening up a small hole in the top. I grinned. My plan was working. I conjured a fireball in my hands and whipped it at the crumbling rubble. I was doing everything in my power to burn, disintegrate, melt, or mold the caved in hallway and create an opening.

"Clay! Give it all you got," shouted Jackson. "We're running out of time."

I initiated another earthquake spell, creating a hole big enough to crawl through at the top of the rubble. I turned around to see how much more time we had and came face to face with the shocking truth.

Time was up.

The golden orb was about to reach us.

This was it.

The wind whistled with the sound of a speeding bullet. Emerging from the ceiling's now open starry space was a rushing blur. It came into sight as it zoomed towards the spirit warden. It was Serena! She had her sword arced, ready to deliver the most insanely powerful crushing blow ever dealt. The sword landed right into the spirit's shoulder, disrupting its self-destruct mode. The golden orb flickered away.

Serena gracefully landed back to the floor, sword in hand. A silver hue surrounded her person, like she was buffed with a special status. She looked up to us, breathing heavily, but smiling a deranged battle-crazed grin. "It's time you guys finally admit you'd be screwed without me."

I rushed towards her and grabbed her in my arms. My chest heaved into hers as I cast healing mist, letting a curative vapor surround our embrace.

"You're still alive," I croaked.

"What is this?" yelled the spirit warden, interrupting our reunion. The golden ethereal substance the guardian was composed of flickered where Serena's blade had landed. "You weren't supposed to come back. No one is supposed to come back."

Serena grinned and turned to us. "You guys need to trust me. Jump into the space. It will be okay. Follow me. It's the only way to defeat the spirit."

Serena ran towards a nearby edge where the temple stone floor met the never-ending starry nebula and cannon-balled into it.

With zero hesitation, Jackson ran and dove into the starry expanse. Kari followed suit. Shade shook his head and approached the edge, turning to me. "Ever since we got a bloody airship mate we've been jumping off cliffs, edges, ships, cities. It's bloody pathological at this point."

I smiled and sprinted to the edge, waving goodbye to the spirit warden as I leapt into the unknown.

A coldness enveloped my body, then a weightlessness. Stars surrounded me. I was pretty sure I was falling but my stomach no longer lurched like it was. My hair didn't fly up. Air didn't rush around me and fill my ears. It felt like I was floating, but I wasn't.

I lifted my hands to my face and saw they were glowing with the same silvery hue surrounding Serena when she crash landed back into the boss battle. A notice appeared on my HUD.

Spirit Armor (Buff): You've been granted spirit armor. Your body is temporarily embedded with ethereal coating, rendering your weapons and attacks capable of inflicting damage on spirits. (Duration: 3 minutes).

"Pretty sweet buff, huh?"
Below me, the rest of my party was all floating down-

ward through the starry sky. Serena was at the bottom of the pack, looking up to us with a smile.

"Defeating this boss requires you to fall through here," said Serena. "The space is a red herring. The real destruction is the spirit warden's blade when it creates the opening, but this space itself is actually key to defeating him."

"Woo! Spirit armor," chanted Shade.

"The counter hasn't even started yet either," observed Kari.

"Nope," said Serena. "It doesn't count down until we land back into the temple chamber."

"Very nice," said Jackson.

Great. We were now prepared to truly duke it out with the spirit warden. Only one question remained.

"How long does this endless floating last?" I said.

"We have another thirty seconds," said Serena. "This space is like a loop, bringing us back to the temple floor. What's left of it anyways."

"We need a plan for when we land," I said. "I say we use the momentum of the fall to land the most amount of sheer DPS we can. Serena you deal another crushing blow. Jackson land with your strongest punch. Shade come at them with mug shot. Kari use whatever your best offensive spell is."

"What are you gonna do?" asked Serena. "It must be tough with all those options."

"Not at all," I grinned. "I know exactly which spell I want."

The temple floor came into view. The spirit warden stood there, idly waiting. Even as we had gained new advantages, he remained still and stoic. Apathetic. He was focused solely on his duty.

I let my hands come close together. My fingers almost

touched, a frosty coolness flowing through them. First a bright blue hilt of ice emerged between my hands, then the long gnarled pointed blade.

I smiled down to Serena. "It looks like I'll be dealing my own version of crushing blow."

"Gets one magic sword and suddenly thinks he's the tank." She grinned at me and turned to Jackson. "The delusions of a glass canon, am-I-right?"

Jackson shook his head with a knowing smirk. He flipped around so he was falling forward with his outstretched arm and fist like Superman.

"Let's go," he said.

His body took on more than a silvery hue. Translucent red flames of energy coursed across his person in jagged lines. His fist crashed into the spirit's chin. The boss' neck twisted to the side, taking a chunk of HP off its health bar.

Shade landed next, digging his daggers into the spirit warden's chest, triggering mugshot. Another chunk of HP fell off. Shade continued to lay a dent into the boss, throwing in stab after stab. He back flipped away right as Serena landed with her crushing blow. The boss was now below 50% HP. The spirit armor made our moves much more effective against the boss than we'd been before.

The floor rushed towards me and I kept the spirit in my sights. I gripped the hilt of my conjured ice blade with both hands. I landed—blade first—on top of the spirit's head.

+Critical Hit!

The boss lifted its glowing arms and knocked me back to the floor, swatting me away like a mere fly. I crashed onto the floor of the chamber, or what was left of it anyway. A sharp pain stretched across my back from the poor landing.

I quickly returned to the fray of battle. The boss' HP was whittling away.

"We're almost there you guys," I said, gripping tightly around my ice blade. "Let's finish this."

I electric blinked right in front of him and stabbed my ice blade—drenched in the silver hue of the spirit armor—right into the spirit's stomach. I twisted the blade and then wrenched it back out.

The warden fell onto his knees. The last bit of his HP ticked away.

"It wasn't supposed to be like this," he said.

"Well, we figured out your trick mate," said Shade.

"Sorry not sorry," said Serena smiling.

"No, you misunderstand me," said the spirit warden. His legs were beginning to disintegrate and fade away into pixelized dust. "No one was supposed to come here. We'd sealed it away. For your own protection. This device will only cause more destruction."

As the spirit warden's whole chest and neck disintegrated, he said his final words: "You have been warned."

"How do you even use it," asked Serena.

"I dunno," said Jackson, peering over.

"Theobold back at Land's Shield will know what to do with it."

"Ah, Land's Shield—how I have forgotten it," mused Shade. "Will we ever get back there and sit in the pub and drink the day away again?"

"You never did that," said Kari.

"I did before I met you ridiculous lot. Always heading off from one adventure to the next. Let's take a break for once. Would that be so bad? Like, right now, why don't we sit down for a picnic? A little glass of wine, perhaps? Or—"

Shade was cut off by the trembling rumble of the floor at our feet. The Lirana raised his finger. "I do not like the sounds of that. Let's get the bloody hell out of here and back to the ship."

The ceiling above us was cracking. Bits of rock and debris fell down from above.

Jackson, Serena and I lifted up the Ultriga Weapon and lumbered it through the crumbling temple, rushing through the hallway by which we came and back up the stairs.

The cool air of the bottom world was refreshing after all the time in the dark dampness of the temple. Yet the earth-quake-like rumble hadn't gone away. The whole hill plat-form we were on, shook and vibrated. The shaking ground went further out too: the dilapidated homes of the city crumbled, broken columns collapsed into walls, crushing them further into ruin.

"Uh oh," said Serena, nodding to the desert beyond Ariellum.

A gust of wind spiraled out in the sea of black sand. The ash drifted across the landscape, revealing a fossilized set of bones. The spiraling wind then did a funny thing. It lifted the bones off the ground. The wind wasn't spiraling furiously in one direction, it was moving each bone individually, reconstructing the fallen fossilized beast. Four sets of feet were created then accompanying legs. Soon the rib cage came together. The wind acted like cartilage, gluing the femurs and others bones together. Next the bones floated beyond the back of the monster, creating a large set of wings. Last but not least was the head, a giant jawed dragon's head with hollow empty eyes of shadow glowing a purple light.

"I guess walking out of here with the Ultriga Weapon wasn't going to be so easy after all," said Shade.

A prompt appeared in my HUD.

New Quest Alert: Escape Ariellum!

A bone dragon has been summoned to protect the Ultriga Weapon from leaving Ariellum. Get back to your ship and exit the bottom world.

Quest Type: Unique
Quest Difficulty: Hard
Time Limit: 3.5 hours (or before the bone dragon finds and kills you)
Reward: 10,000 EXP
Accept: Yes/No ?

"Run!" I yelled, accepting the quest and dashing down the outer steps of the acropolis, heading back the way we came. The footsteps and heavy breaths of the others echoed behind me. They were drowned out by the ferocious roar of the bone dragon.

We hurried down the steps of the acropolis. Thankfully,

there were no fallen soldiers waiting for our return. We focused on running the hell away from the giant bone dragon chasing behind us. Its flapping wings created a gale of wind against my back. Its roar made my whole body tremble.

Jackson and I were holding the front of the Ultriga Weapon while Serena and Shade held the backside of it. Kari covered us from behind, keeping tabs on the bone dragon.

"Ugh, why is this thing so heavy?" groaned Shade.

"It can literally destroy the entire Illyrian continent," said Serena, red in the face from lifting her end of the relic weapon. "Of course a device that powerful is going to be ridiculously heavy!"

"It's gaining on us guys," said Kari.

"We're not going to be able to outrun this thing while carrying this," said Jackson.

"Alright then," I said. "Let's drop it and face this thing head on."

We placed the Ultriga Weapon down and turned around to fight the bone dragon. The giant deathly creature roared and swooped down towards us. Its open jaw filled with purple arcane flames.

"Get back!" I yelled.

We all dove down the stairs as the dragon unleashed a wave of purple flames across the steps of the acropolis.

We managed to dodge the attack, but the flames surrounded the Ultriga Weapon. Smoke wafted across the steps. We waited to see if the relic item we'd fought so hard to acquire was still intact. When the smoke cleared, the Ultriga Weapon sat right where we had left it, good as new.

Of course. The ancient device was too powerful to be destroyed by normal means.

"I don't see how we can beat this thing," said Serena. "How will we even get in range so we can attack it?"

"Don't be so pessimistic," I said. "Watch."

I ran and jumped in the air, creating a pool of mana at my feet. I jumped again and again after that. I ignored how high I was suspended in the air and focused on the bone dragon swirling in the sky nearby. It saw me coming towards it and zoomed straight at me.

"That's right," I said.

I jumped again and stretched out my arm towards the dragon. My palm opened wide and I let forth a sparkling chain whip of lightning. It wrapped itself around the bone dragon's right leg.

It squirmed at the new paralysis of the lightning cage, pulsing and throbbing into its bone leg.

I held onto the chain of lightning and let myself fall back to the ground, dragging the bone dragon by the leg. The ground approached and I created another pool of mana at the bottom of my feet to cushion my final landing.

I was on the ground for a second when the dragon yanked its tail and brought me back afloat.

Jackson ran across the platform and tackled me in the air, using his muscle and weight to pin me and the lightning chain down. The heavy-set Rorn was like an anchor.

"Give it all you got," yelled Jackson. "This is our opportunity to really weaken it."

"Here goes nothing," yelled Serena, charging towards the bone dragon, sword raised. Bullets from Shade's pistols zoomed past her shoulders racing to hit the ghastly creature ahead of her. The bullets bounced off the bone, barely dealing any damage, but Serena didn't let it slow her down. She leapt in the air, sword raised, and unleashed crushing blow right where the wings sprouted from the dragon's body. The blade crushed through the bones, snapping the wing off with ease.

The bone dragon roared. It lost its balance as one wing fell into the ruins of Ariellum. It still dragged and attempted to escape the grasp of my chain lightning. I was still hanging onto it tight. Yet the spell was coming to an end. I only had thirty more seconds until I'd have to cast it again.

I threw out my other arm and let a new rope of electricity burst forth from my hands. The spell was met with a shrill cry from the bone dragon. The monster shot out a blast of purple flame. The two spells clashed with each other in the air and cancelled one another out.

Damn.

Now I was locked out of the move for another thirty seconds. The dragon had more than enough time to fly off. Or hobble away given it was missing a wing.

My lightning chain dissipated and the bone dragon wasted no time in flying away. It landed further up the platform of stairs. It curled up like a dog licking its wounds. I was about to suggest picking up the Ultriga Weapon again when the magical force that had manipulated its bones went to work, repairing its broken wing.

"This thing is operating like the skeleton warriors we fought before," I said. "What about healing magic?"

"Already tried," said Kari. "It didn't do anything."

With its wings repaired, the dragon flew towards us. It hissed and shrieked. The bones rattled and knocked against each other with every flap of its wings or craning of its neck.

We all retreated down the steps. The bone dragon swooped down. Serena stood at the front our party, holding her sword up horizontally, triggering sword shield.

The bone dragon didn't attack us though. It swooped down and clawed the Ultriga Weapon and flew away.

"Wait what," said Serena.

"This goes against all my previous burglary experience," said Shade. "Guard dogs usually care more about getting their supper than actually capturing whatever has been stolen."

"If we want to keep the Ultriga Weapon," said Jackson. "We have to fight the bone dragon. The question is: how badly do we want it?"

"I can't believe you guys," I said. "We jumped through an interdimensional warp while fighting the spirit warden to get this thing and now you're ready to give up at a mere bone dragon."

"I mean, I wouldn't say 'mere'," said Shade.

I shook my head and materialized an MP potion. I uncorked it and guzzled it down. "Do we want to save Illyria or not. This is the only way."

I ran after the dragon, electric blinking into the air. Then again and again. I shot off lightning cage which grabbed hold of its leg. I swung through the air attached to the dragon. It squealed and shook from the pain of my lightning whip. In it's pain it let go of the Ultriga Weapon. The device fell through the air and smashed into the staircase. I let go of my lightning grip and fell back to the ground, cushioning my fall at the last second.

I stood in the crumbling stairwell, beside the Ultriga Weapon. The rest of the party ran up to me.

"We need to fight for this thing," I said. "Even if its against a monstrosity like the bone dragon."

The rest of the party readied themselves for a fight once again.

The dragon swerved in the air and set its deadly purple eyes on us. It flapped its wings and glided downwards across the wretched gray sky of the bottom world.

Serena ran up the steps ready to meet its attack. The dragon whipped out its clawed arms, swiping them across the sky at the warrior. Serena leapt and initiated blade tornado, spinning through the air, cutting into the bone structure of the dragon.

Jackson ran and leapt towards the dragon, doing a spin kick into its skull, knocking out its crumbling bone teeth.

Kari enchanted both of them with defensive and offensive buffs.

The bone dragon craned its neck upward, letting out a shrill wail. It then whipped its head down, hot breath gusting out of its mouth and knocking all of us back a step. A massive blast of purple flame shot forth from its throat . We were surrounded by the arcane flames. The hair on my skin melted away. My flesh warped from the heat of the blast.

I lifted up both my arms and shot out waterblast from my palms, drenching and suffocating the surrounding flames. The dragon took a normal breath and arched its head back. Residual flames lingered on the stone steps of the acropolis.

We were all in the red and the dragon was about to unleash another blast.

Serena turned and ran from the dragon. "Everybody run," she yelled.

"But—"

"Enough is enough," said Serena, body tackling me and sending the two of us rolling down the steps. The stones banged into my back and shoulder blades, bones painfully clapping against the cold ancient steps.

We stopped rolling and I stood up. "What the hell Serena?"

"I'm not going back for the stupid bloody weapon

anymore. It's only going to get us killed. Don't you see that Clay?"

The dragon flew down to where the Ultriga Weapon was and picked it up with its claws and flew away with it.

I ran after it again, but Serena gripped my arm, halting me.

"I know you want to save everyone, but don't you see this isn't the way? You care so much about protecting everyone you'll do anything to do it. You're blinded. You want to save everyone so badly you'll let yourself and the rest of us get killed because of it. How can we help anyone then? Don't go after the weapon. We don't need it. There's gotta be another way."

The dragon flapped its wings, taking the Ultriga Weapon deeper into the sky with it. If I ran now I had a chance to catch up with it. Any further and it was gone. It was now or never.

Serena's sharp blue eyes locked onto mine. I had almost lost her in the battle with the spirit warden. I honestly thought I had. I didn't want to ever go through such pain and misery again. My shoulders fell. She was right.

"Let's go everyone," I said. "We're aborting the current mission."

Everyone's faces fell. No one wanted to fight the dragon anymore. No one believed we were strong enough to beat it.

We'd placed all our hopes of salvation in the Ultriga Weapon. What were we going to do?

The bone dragon was nothing but a speck in the sky now.

"I'm not so sure," said Shade. "Clay—what is your brilliant idea?"

I grinned. "Sorry to say it doesn't involve promoting you Shade, but it might save our bacon."

"Go on," said Jackson, crossing his arms.

"Back when I played RPGs as a kid, there was always a room before the big boss. It usually had a save point. I was in such a rush as a kid I always ended up being severely underleveled. The great thing about this room though was you were able to stay in it as long as you wanted. It was even possible to backtrack to earlier areas you'd been to. The room allowed you to grind and level up and make the necessary arrangements needed before fighting the big boss. Right now—here in the bottom world—is our version of that room. We're not ready to exit and face our enemies. Yet."

"We only have three more hours left down here before the bottom world sickness overtakes us. Plus, I don't know if grinding levels will be enough," said Jackson.

I shook my head and smiled. "Neither do I. I specifically want to grind just one of my spells. It might be the key to winning the fight against Arethkar."

∾

"I'M JUST SUPPOSED to stand here and take it," balked Shade, standing alone and isolated on the black desert sand.

"All of us are," said Jackson, a good few meters away from Shade. Serena stood even further out.

"I don't see Kari or Clay doing this bloody fool's work," complained Shade.

"C'mon Shade," said Serena. "You know why we're doing this."

Shade sighed and pulled out his pistol. "Yeah, yeah, yeah. Let's get this started." He fired his pistol out into the desert floor. Within seconds, sand sharks sensed the movement and were coming our way.

"Just because I understand why we're doing it, doesn't mean I have to like it," said Shade, squirming.

"Just close your eyes and let it happen," said Jackson calmly.

The ground shook as the sand sharks made their approach. They jumped out of the sand and whipped their tails at our frontline.

Jackson, Shade, and Serena all fell back, purposely not defending themselves. A little icon for "stunned" flickered beneath their status bars.

Here we go. I electric blinked closer to the battle field, then stretched out my arm. I shot off a bright light of crystal energy towards Shade. Then Serena. Then Jackson. The status debuff disappeared from beneath their status bars. Kari followed up my spell with cure magic of her own.

"Okay guys," I said, panting. "Again."

We did this loop, over and over again for another two hours. By the end of the grind, we'd leveled up Status Cure to level 10. I was now "medically trained" to cure: poison, confusion, slow, weakness, paralysis, chilled, fear, burning, crippled, shock, bio, and berserk.

Loads of potential debuffs but not the one we wanted.

"We're running out of time, Clay," said Serena.

She was right. We only had forty minutes before the gates sealed shut forever. It was also taking more and more time to level up the skill. It would take at least twenty-five minutes to level it up again. Were we wasting our time here? No. We had enough time to level up status cure once more. I was feeling lucky.

"We're trying one more time," I said. "Everyone stay in positions, let's go."

The sand sharks returned and knocked Shade back, stunning him for the two hundredth time. I ran and healed him from the attack. Kari brought his HP back to full after I cured him of the debuff. I ran over to Serena next, then Jackson. We continued this dance for another twenty minutes. The whole time I worried what if the next level—level 11—didn't unlock the debuff we needed. What then? I shook my head. I had to believe. I had to hope, even if I knew unlocking the ability did not ensure the success of the plan. Part two—if we ever got so far—would solve the remaining issues.

I cured Serena from her stunned state, the bright crystals of the spell seeping into her skin and removing the debuff. A message flickered in my HUD.

Status Cure has leveled up (Level 11)
Status Cure: Remove debuffs ailing you and your party members. Removable debuffs include: poison, confusion, slow, weakness, stun, chilled, fear, burning, crippled, shock, bio, berserk, and enslaved (new!)

I grinned. We had done it.

"We did it," I yelled.

"Hurrah!" said Shade. "Can we stop being practice dummies and finish off these sand sharks?"

"There's no time," said Serena. "Let's retreat and they'll eventually give up on chasing us."

"Fine," groaned Shade.

Jackson did a spinning kick and sent an incoming sand shark meters across the desert floor. He landed and dusted off his trousers. "I hate to be the barer of bad news but I'm not sure if this spell is going to be enough. If I were still wearing my slave's bracers, even if you cast the spell on me and removed the debuff, it would only last a millisecond, not even that. The bracers would constantly keep the debuff active."

"I thought of that," I said. "That's why we need to initiate part two of my plan."

I was going to unlock my tier-2 class.

I'd been avoiding doing this for a long time. It was easier to wait and figure out later what the best class was, what the sweetest moves were, but really all I'd been doing was procrastinating. Here I was: about to face the battle dictating Illyria's future and my future in it and I was hoarding class skill points. WTF. I was being idiotic. It was time to pick my next class. They were all interesting and I had enough to unlock any of the four available to me, but I needed to pick based, not on some future where I leveled up and found cool unique moves, but what was going to save our asses right here and now. That made the choice a lot easier.

We needed allies. We needed more fighters. If I could somehow get more of them, I had to do whatever was in my power to do so.

I was going to become a Summoner.

I placed four class skill points to unlock the two prerequisite moves for summoner class. I put two points into the utility branch of Fire magic, learning "Ring of Fire" and "Summon Phoenix." Next I put two points into Earth magic utility branch, learning "Spike Field" and "Summon Rock Golem."

As soon as I learned "Summon Rock Golem," a message appeared in my prompt.

You're now eligible to embark on quest trials for: mage and summoner. Select at any time.

"Okay guys," I said, looking at my team. "Wait right here. I will be back in a second."

I opened up my class screen and selected the summoner quest trial.

Would you like to embark on, "Summoner Quest Trial"? Y/N?

I selected yes and instantly everything went black. I opened my eyes and I was somewhere else. The black desert sand cushioning against the sole of my boots was replaced by the cold stone floor of an ancient temple. The whistle of the harsh wind was replaced by the gentle rustle of green vine leaves against the stone windows of the ziggurat. The temple was similar to the one I'd visited when I had unlocked my apprentice mage class. A whole bunch of messages stacked in my HUD.

Summoner Class Kit Temporarily Unlocked

A student of spirit and eternal essences, you summon creatures to fight and battle on your behalf.

Effect 1: +500 MP
Effect 2: 10% Faster MP Regeneration

Effect 3: Bind Summon Skill Unlocked
Effect 4: Summon Bound Spirit Unlocked
Effect 5: Summon Elemental Spirit Unlocked
Effect 6: Summoner Arsenal Slot 1 Unlocked
Effect 7: Summoner Arsenal Slot 2 Unlocked
Effect 8: Summoner Arsenal Slot 3 Unlocked

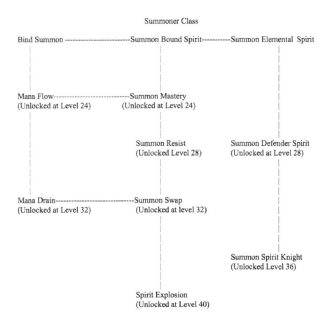

Holy crap. This was a lot to take in. I wasn't even sure where to start. Before pouring over the skill tree, I took in the bonus effects for unlocking the class. 500 MP! That was seriously a truck load. I bet it was because summoning would cost a lot of mana, but still, the bonus MP was worth it enough to unlock this class and then switch to another. How many classes were you allowed to unlock?

Dynamic Class System – Primary and Sub Classes

A player can only ever have the abilities and status upgrades of two classes at once. However, classes that are sequentially linked via tiers, such as "Apprentice Mage" (Tier-1) and "Summoner" (Tier-2) are considered only one class. Thus a player could have "Summoner" (with "Apprentice Mage" abilities falling under that class) and another class like "Warrior" or "Paladin", thus effectively controlling three classes at one time. However, only one branching tier-1 and tier-2 class count as one (i.e. it would count as two classes to have both summoner and medic-mage open at once).

Interesting. You weren't able to have three separate classes open at once. Yet, theoretically you were still able to have loads of classes and their abilities at your disposal so long as those classes were sequentially linked. So it was possible to have up to five or six classes at your disposal if you had multiple tier-3 classes unlocked. But how did you unlock tier-3 classes? I waited for the HUD to display a prompt explaining this to me, but nothing came up. Huh? I guess going from tier-2 to tier-3 would be different than tier-1 to tier-2. I'd have to ask Theobold or someone about this later.

I looked over the skill tree; I currently had unlocked the first set of three skills on the tree. Judging by the skills there were two clearly distinctive play styles for this class. There was a zerg-style available, meaning summon-as-many-small-creatures-to-overwhelm-your-enemy method of fighting. Or, alternatively, a more familiar-based curated Summoner who had a limited amount of creatures to

"Are you being sarcastic?"

The spirit frowned. "Did I upset master? I didn't mean to!"

"Agh, okay, never mind. You didn't upset me. We're running out of time before you disappear. Speaking of which, how long will I have to wait to recast you again?"

"Great question, new master summoner! At level one, I believe it will be five minutes."

"Wow okay. I don't want to waste any time. Can you do me a favor and go over there and pull that lever."

"Sure," it said and squeezed through the bars and floated across the room to the lever. "This one right here?"

"Yes!"

The spirit spun around the lever and pushed it to the other end. The bars lifted. There was still thirty seconds on the clock. This spirit—despite its pathological over enthusiasm for everything—was super helpful already. It gave me an idea.

"Hey! I might need your help throughout the rest of the trial. Is it alright if I bind summon you so you can stay out here and help me for longer?"

The elemental spirit was taken aback. "Really? You'd do me such an honor. You'd place me—a lowly elemental spirit—in your prized arsenal?"

"You'd be the first. What do you say?"

"I accept!"

Elemental Spirit has joined your summoning arsenal. You now have 2 out of 3 arsenal slots remaining.

I checked the elemental spirits stats and they had changed.

Elemental Spirit
Level 1
Summoning Duration: 24 hours

Oh wow. A bound creature was able to stay out much longer than the lesser summons. This was perfect. I'd need this enthusiastic spirit's help if I were to complete these trials. Speaking of which, it needed a new name.

"Hey, what if I gave you a nickname?" I said. "How does Chip sound? Because, you know, you're so chipper."

"Wowee! First you bound me to your summoner arsenal and then you gift me personal nickname of friendship," said the spirit, swirling around me. "I love it. Call me Chip, master summoner!"

I stepped into the new room now that the bars were gone. The elemental spirit spiraled around my person, chanting some kind of song.

"Master and Spirit working together / Solving Puzzles / Having a great time!"

"Yeah I'm having a great time too. Can you stop singing please?"

"Sure thing master. I'll be silent. I'll do whatever. Say the word and I'll do it. Like right now: you asked for quiet and I gave it to you. Zipped it. Shut it. Not a peep. Not a whistle. Not a sound—"

I crossed my arms and stared at the spirit. It stopped talking.

"Do you have any idea what's behind this door?"

The spirit shook its head.

"You actually don't know or are you hoping to please me by staying quiet?"

The spirit nodded its head. Then shook it. Then

frowned in confusion. "I don't know what's behind the door," it finally said.

Okay. It was time to find out then I supposed. I pushed the wooden door opened and entered the new room. It was full of mechanical spiders, clicketing and clacketing along the room. At the other end was a door. I took another step and the floor in front of me completely disintegrated and fell, opening a big gaping hole to the sky. The clickety-clacking mechanical spiders all fell through the air with the floor.

I turned to the elemental spirit. "Hey, you can fly, can I hold onto you?"

"I wish you were able to master but you can't because I'm immaterial!"

"Will you do me a favor and float to the other side where that door is? Come back and tell me what you see over there."

The spirit nodded its head and flew across the empty air to the other side. It paced across the floor, taking everything in and flew back to me.

"What did you see?"

"A platform like this one with a door," it said.

"Was there a lever or a switch like in the other room?"

"I didn't see one. Did you want me to check again?"

I shook my head. It wouldn't be useful. I rubbed my chin in thought. I jumped off the platform. I smashed into an invisible wall. The force field wouldn't let me go forward. This was a test to become a summoner, so using my other abilities wasn't what I was supposed to do here.

A clickety-clack came from nearby. The only two surviving mechanical spiders were climbing across the wall on the vertical end.

Interesting.

They crawled along the wall until they reached our platform and slowly clawed onto the horizontal flooring.

"I think I found my way across," I said.

"Yay!" said the elemental spirit, spinning around me.

I approached the spiders. Binding the spirit had been easy, but I'd faced these spiders before. They were hostile.

"How do I bind hostile things?" I said, turning to Chip.

"You have to earn their respect through a variety of combat and fear. If you get them below 20% HP, you will be able to bind them easily."

"Great, thanks Chip."

"No problem. I don't know why they're so hostile. You're the best!"

I smirked. Chip was growing on me. "You need to teach my other pals how to be more supportive."

"Sure! I'd be happy to."

My joke had flown over the spirit's head.

"Alright, we'll talk more later, but right now, wanna help me weaken these mechanical spiders?"

"Sure!"

The spirit flew towards the mechanical spiders and unleashed its energy attack. The spiders crawled towards it and jumped in the air, but flew right through it.

"Ha! Silly spiders," said the spirit. "I'm immaterial!"

I stretched out my arms and threw my hand out, letting a lightning whip emanate from my palm. The blue lightning streaked across the platform, wrapping itself around the mechanical spider, caging it in its coil. The mecha spider squirmed in the lightning grip: both paralyzed and damaging itself as the electricity throbbed into it.

"You can conjure lightning!?" said Chip with awed disbelief. "That's so cool!"

I grinned, conjuring a fireball in the palm of my hands. "Want to see more cool spells?"

I whipped the ball of molten lava at the paralyzed mecha spider. It squirmed in pain from its paralyzed state.

"Whoah! Amazing!"

The other spider jump attacked Chip again. The spirit shot another projectile blast at it, knocking it against the wall.

I threw out more standard fireballs and the creatures both fell below 20% HP. I ran up to the first one and waited for a prompt to appear.

"Touch its head Clay," said Chip. "Then it will sense you want to bind with it."

I put my head down on the mechanical spider and a prompt appeared.

Would you like to use bind summon on this mecha spider? Y/N?

I selected yes and the spider disappeared in a silvery essence.

You now have one remaining spot in your summoner arsenal (2/3)

I went over to the other mecha spider, scurrying away. I placed my hand on its head and repeated the process again. When I was finished a prompt appeared telling me my summoner arsenal was full.

"Alright, I gotta get both those spiders back out here. They're going to help me cross this chasm."

I stretched out my hands and cast summon bound spirit. A silver air glowed at my feet and the mecha spider reappeared. I did it again and both were there. I checked their stats.

Mecha Spider
Level 1
Abilities: Claw attack, jump, grapple
Duration: 24 hours

I picked up both metal spiders with my hands, gripping onto their abdomens. I then placed them on the walls. Their metal feet dug into the stone and gripped themselves there.

"Perfect," I said and pulled them out. "Now let's see if they can carry my weight."

I jumped up and placed one spider up and it dug into the wall. I dangled half a foot off the ground. I swung my arm with the other spider and had it latch onto the wall. "Alright, here we go," I said. "Spiders crawl along the wall to the other side."

The spider moved their pincer legs across the wall, sticking to it and dragging me across.

"Chip," I said. "Meet me on the other side. I don't want you distracting me while I'm hanging over the middle of empty sky."

The spiders crawled along and I gripped on their abdomens. Don't look down, I kept telling myself. I didn't feel too panicked about my current state, with death waiting below me if I were to fall. No—I had the curious satisfaction of solving a dungeon puzzle.

When we got to the other side, I let go of the spiders.

"Yay, you did it!" said Chip, spinning around me.

I looked over the long chasm I'd climbed across and sighed. *Yeah, I had.* My stomach dropped. I didn't want to think of it anymore.

On to the next room. Chip spun around me and the little mecha spiders clicked and clacked behind me following along.

I entered the next room and found a familiar face. The floating spirit from my apprentice mage trial. It was a skinny spirit figure with a cloak hiding its face. It grinned, revealing a set of small pointy teeth.

"So you're done being an apprentice then?"

I didn't speak right away. Was this the final room then? I'd met this guy before in the final room of the apprentice mage trials. He had tested me on my philosophy of magic. Only when I had answered his question correctly had he allowed me to pass and unlock my class.

"A summoner is a powerful class," said the ghost. "You can raise whole armies or lead a band of powerful legendary creatures. If it is indeed your choice, select one of the three mystic companions to begin your journey as a summoner."

The spirit faded away and in his place appeared three different amazing creatures. There was a lion-like creature with red hair and sharp claws. A massive translucent blue spirit wolf. The third creature was a large alligator-like monster.

"Which one are you going to pick, Clay?" asked Chip. "I like the lion!"

The lion was cool. I approached the beast. It didn't move or roar. It stood calmly like a toy animal.

A prompt appeared in my HUD.

Mystic Lion
Level 1
The mystic lion is renowned for its strength in battle. If you seek a companion to fight at your side, you'll find a no better warrior in the mystic lion.

Sweet. So the mystic lion was a battle companion. I moved over to the spirit wolf.

Mystic Wolf
Level 1
The Mystic Wolf is known in legends for its great speed.
If you wish to travel across great swathes of land, the
Mystic Wolf is a strong choice for travel companion.

Wow. So the mystic wolf was like a really cool summonable mount then. This was exciting.

I walked over to the alligator creature. I had already discounted it in my head because in appearances it was the weakest and oddest of the three companions.

Mystic Croc
Level One
The Mystic Croc is king of the swamp. If you seek treasure or worlds hidden in the middle of lakes, seas, and oceans—the mystic croc can help you get there.

Oh nice. So this was a water-based mount. I didn't think it would let me breath underwater or anything, but it did traverse big seas which sounded pretty cool.

"Claaaay! Which one are you gonna choose?" said Chip, spinning around the room. "I can't take the suspense."

I wasn't sure. Was I missing anything? The freaky spirit wizard had left me to make my choice. I was only allowed to pick one.

It also meant I'd have to let go of one of my three summoner arsenal. I was obviously keeping Chip so it meant bye-bye to one of the mecha spiders.

Beyond the three creatures was a crack in the wall. I

walked over to it. I winced and peered through the division to see what was on the other side. There was another room.

What the hell?

"Hey Chip," I said. "Do you mind slipping through this crack here and seeing what's on the other side?"

"I'd love to," grinned Chip, floating through the air and then slipping between the walls. Seconds later, he re-emerged.

"There is another room with a door with a weird symbol on it," said Chip. "Also there's a lever in there like in the other room."

My eyes widened. "Really? Chip can you go back and pull the lever."

The spirit nodded eagerly and went back to the hidden room. The walls moved apart, creating a passageway.

This was amazing. I'd stumbled onto a secret area most players didn't normally reach. It must have been a small reward for bounding Chip to my arsenal. Most players probably summoned him and let him disappear and didn't have the patience to wait around to resummon him again.

I walked down the newly formed hallway and approached a large brown wooden door. My stomach dropped when I stood face to face with the entrance to the secret room. I was no longer sure if I'd entered a secret area for savvy players or rather accidentally stepped into a forbidden zone, not meant for anybody.

Etched on the doorway was the same symbol branded on my wrist.

The Prophetic Seal.

"I'm not sure if we should go through here Chip," I said.

"Really?" said the spirit, spinning in a wide circle around me. "Aren't you curious what's in there? I know I am!"

I mean, who was I kidding? I really wanted to know

what was in there, but how did I open this thing? Did I need a special line of code like the other Prophetic Seal skills?

Whatever was beyond here must have been really special. It was already hidden from behind those walls plus it had an extra layer of defense only programmers of the game had access to.

I approached the door and placed my hand against it. A hot sharp pain shot out from my wrist. I screamed from the shock of agonizing hurt.

The Prophetic Seal on the door glowed, sensing the presence of the mark on my person. The doors swung open, revealing the hidden chamber.

The room before me was half collapsed. Bright light shone through holes in the ceiling, casting a silvery spotlight on the rubble and broken floors.

Standing in the center of the room was a majestic looking creature. It had white fur and wings. Its face was like an owl but with pointy ears and a large beak. Holy crap. It was gryphon!

As I got closer, a prompt appeared in my HUD.

Gryphon
Level 1
An old and legendary bird. In ancient Illyria, gryphon riders were only ridden by the strongest most elite summoners.

My eyes widened. I had hit the jackpot. The three creatures in the previous room were cool, but none of them beat a freaking gryphon.

I cracked my knuckles. "Time to bound this spirit."

Chip rushed in front of me, floating through my body as he did so.

"That felt really weird," I said. "Can you not do that again?"

"Sorry Clay! I promise to never float through you again. I have taken note that it is considered a faux-pas amongst materialized people."

"Okay, apology noted."

"Thank you Clay! You see, I slipped through you to stop you from approaching the gryphon. Unlike the mystic creatures of the other realm, you'll most likely have to battle this gryphon to bind it to your summoner arsenal."

I paused. I didn't want to actively hurt this gorgeous majestic creature, but I didn't want to walk away from this opportunity either. If I had to battle it, I would. I'd try and bind it peacefully first though.

I took a step towards the gryphon. Its head poked up, alert. Its hazel eyes stared into mine.

"Hi," I said, feeling like a total dumbass. How was I supposed to talk to a gryphon? "You're a strong and powerful creature. I seek an ally such as yourself."

An ally or a slave?

I stumbled back a step. Did I hear the creature speak to me?

"Did you hear that Chip?"

"Hear what Clay?"

I turned to the gryphon. "Did you speak into my mind?"

Yes. Now answer my question.

"I wouldn't seek to harm you," I said. "I'd want you to fight alongside me for noble causes. I want an ally, not a slave."

Such words are easier to say before I am bound to you and cannot leave your control.

"Well, what if we made a deal. You become a bound summon of mine and, say, if you ever wanted to leave my company, I'd let you do so, no questions asked. You'll have fun with me and my party—more fun than up here in this crumbly room."

Gryphons don't live for fun.

"Sure, but think about all the fish and game to taste and try in all the places we will venture to."

The bird's brow peaked. It may not have lived for fun, but it certainly lived for meat.

I still don't trust you.

"Here," I said and materialized a slab of sand shark meat from earlier and tossed it over to the gryphon. The creature stretched out its neck and gobbled up the meat. The gryphon then spoke to me once more.

I like your offer and the conditions you propose. I will accept such a bound request.

Congratulations! You've learned new passive Summoner ability: Contract Negotiations.

Every bound summon enters a contract with its summoner; for most, it's a standard contract for life. Yet for legendary and powerful creatures that cannot be defeated so easily, it may be worth it to negotiate the summoner contract.

Do you wish to bound Gryphon to your summoner arsenal? Y/N?*
*(Special Summoner Contract enforced: Gryphon is allowed to leave Summoner's Arsenal if it wishes)

I turned to the gryphon. "How do I know you won't abandon me mid-battle or screw me over somehow?"

The gryphon shook its head. *You don't, but gryphons*

aren't known to be swindlers. Also, you're the first out of all the many summoners who've approached me to suggest such a noble proposal: that we are allies in battle, rather than master and slave. I'm not a pony you ride, but a friend you seek for aid. You interest me, human, and so far, have my respect.

I guess that was his version of: take my word for it, I won't screw you over.

I clicked "yes" in my HUD and a new message appeared.

Alert! Summoner Arsenal Over Occupied (4/3). Please set free one bound summon.

Uh-oh. I chose to set free one of the mecha spiders. It clicked and clacked away from me. It was lonely by itself. All the other mecha spiders had fallen away with the previous room's trap. I set free the other mecha spider so I wasn't separating the two of them. They clacked away into the other room.

The gryphon was no longer in front of me. It had disappeared. It now existed in a nether realm of familiars.

The floating old wizard reappeared in the room.

"An interesting choice," said the wizard. "You have proven yourself to summon elemental spirits and have them do your bidding. Make alliances with unlikely creatures to help you solve your problems and wise enough to negotiate contracts with creatures far beyond your power. For proving all of this, I hereby grant you the powers of a summoner!"

Class Unlocked: Summoner!

"Congratulations Clay!" cheered Chip. "I knew you could do it."

I smiled at the elemental spirit. "Thanks dude. Keep it

mind this may have been the easiest part of today. This trial is like an oasis from where we're heading back to."

"Oh no!"

"That's right Chip," I said, walking towards a portal that replaced the freaky wizard. "Prepare yourself for a world of shit."

33

I emerged back on the deck of the *Horizon's Dream*. The gray skies of the bottom world lingered overhead. The cool breeze brushed against my skin. The party stood exactly where I had been standing when I'd pressed the portal scroll.

"Um, have you guys been standing here the whole time?"

Serena's eyebrows furrowed. "What do you mean the whole time? You haven't done anything."

"Whoah! Cool ship Clay! Are these your other best friends?"

Chip flew out from underneath my feet and zoomed around the mainmast of the *Horizon's Dream*.

"Back off foul spirit," yelled Shade, whipping out his pistol.

"No Shade! He's with me."

"Oh, really? Can he float through us? Now that would be a cool parlor trick for the pub."

Chip floated up to Shade. "Clay told me not to float

through him. He said it was a faux-pas against materially substantive persons. May I float through you?"

"Go for it," said Shade, shrugging.

The spirit floated through him and the Lirana thief giggled. "Tickles!"

Serena and Jackson stared with disbelief at the happy ghost and thief getting along and then back to me. Their faces were unimpressed.

"I see your class has changed," said Jackson. "So you must've entered a different temporal zone from here when you entered the trial. Interesting. Regardless, well-done on unlocking your class. Is this ghost your main companion?"

"His name is Chip and no, I wouldn't say he's my main. Actually, I was able to form a bond with a gryphon."

"A gryphon!" said Kari, eyes-wide.

Chip flew over to Kari. "Yeah! It was so cool. The gryphon was all like, 'I don't want to be allies with you' and then Clay was like, 'C'mon gryphon, I'm the best' and then the gryphon was convinced."

"Cool story, bro," said Serena. She turned to me. "Is, uhh, Chip over here aware of our current situation?"

"Yes ma'am," said the elemental spirit. "Clay said we were about to walk into a world of shit, but to tell you the truth, I only see black sand."

"Chip—I know you're excited but I need you to calm down," I said. "When I said world of shit, I meant a world of metaphorical shit."

Chip's small black eyes widened. "You mean immaterial shit? Like me."

"Sort of like you, but even more immaterial. Like non-existent. Figurative. To rephrase what I initially meant was: there's real bad people who want to hurt us beyond the gates of this world. In a second, I'm going to open them up and we're going to face those people. The battle is going to be long and grueling and I'm going to need you to fight and help me with even more strength than you showed me in the trial temple. Understand?"

The spirit nodded.

I looked up to the rest of the team. "We've done all the preparation we can. It's time to face Captain Kaige. It's time to face Arethkar. It's time we ended this fight."

Everybody cheered and assumed positions. I turned to Serena and said, "It's time we tried the other way."

34

//Run:Open_DLC_Content

The words transformed into an inky black blast of magic from my hands, opening up the gates of the bottom world once more to greater Illyria. Jackson ignited the engine and blasted the ship through the newly opened portal.

The bright blue skies of the cloud ocean were in sight, a mere arm's reach away. It was a deception though, part of the magic. My stomach stretched, my teeth ached, and my ears popped as our ship traversed the dimensional tunnel.

The ship shook and vibrated, arriving back in the skies of Argon's Rage. The situation was as we had left it. Or partially as we had left it. There was not a Sky Wyrm in sight. The Arethkarian fleet, greeting us with its turrets and cannons, had taken care of the other threats while we'd been away. They'd been waiting idly for us to return.

A crew member ran up to me, holding a crystal transmission device. "Captain! The fleet is making contact with us, sir!"

"Bring the communication crystal over here then."

I took the crystal out of the crew member's trembling hands. I'd managed to raise the morale up to neutral before we'd embarked, but the fear being stoked by the sheer number of the Arethkarian fleet, was hard to swallow.

"Captain Hopewell," spoke Oren Kaige from the crystal transmitter. "I'm sure you can see you're vastly outnumbered. Hand over the Ultriga Weapon and we'll show you mercy."

"I wonder what mercy from slave traders looks like," said Shade. "Why don't you ask him?"

"I don't know why you're acting like you hold all the cards here Oren," I said. "We now control the greatest weapon ever created in Illyria. How about you listen to our terms? Retreat back to the shores of your continent. Take your fleet and armada with you. Sign a peace treaty."

Laughter transmitted from the crystal. Our whole ship was silent, listening in fearful captivation of the manic cackle echoing through the crystal.

"Here's something I've learned about you Captain Hopewell. Why I wasn't afraid when you entered the bottom world and sealed the opening from us. Even if you got your hands on the bloody Ultriga Weapon—you wouldn't have the guts to use it. You're not someone who pulls the trigger. It's the fundamental difference between you and me. I'll do what it takes to save my people. You—you're nothing but hot air."

I was sick of listening to this asshole talk. It was time to put our plan into action.

I stretched out both my arms and cast summon bound spirit. Gryph emerged, neighing its beak.

"Is that your freaking bound spirit," said Jackson, taken aback.

"That's right, bitches," I said. "Clay Hopewell has got a motherfucking gryphon. Now let's initiate the plan."

Oren Kaige was still yammering about how much I sucked via the crystal transmitter which I let slip into my pocket. I walked over to Gryph. "Hello again, ally of mine. If it's alright with you, would it be okay if we mutually agreed I ride on your back and you help me kick these lame guys' asses?"

Certainly. The gryphon dipped its neck in front of me. *Get on.*

The rest of the party looked at me funny.

"What?"

"It's just you have a weird relationship," said Serena. "Why were you talking to it so politely?"

"It's like, the gryphon is in charge, not you?" said Jackson.

"All hail captain gryphon," said Shade. "Ask it if I can be first mate?"

"Alright, stop chirping me," I said. "Let's initiate the plan."

I grabbed the reins of the gryphon and we kicked off the deck of the ship and flew into the clouds.

The wind of the open air blew my hair back and I gripped on tightly to the gryphon's back.

"That doesn't hurt, does it?"

No. It is less than a pinch. Nothing.

I pulled back on the gryphon when we were midway between the *Horizon's Dream* and the Arethkarian fleet. I grabbed the transmission crystal from my pocket and found Oren Kaige still yammering into it.

"Alright Captain Kaige, you convinced me," I said into the crystal. I summoned Chip and then the fiery phoenix. I gestured with my finger on my mouth to be quiet.

"Hrmph. I wasn't expecting you to be so reasonable. How about you lower your cannons and turrets and let us board your ship?"

I cast status cure over and over again. I spun my finger in the air and both Chip and the phoenix knew what I wanted them to do. Gryph followed their lead. I kept casting status cure over and over again, creating a field of golden glowing crystals, all swept up in a spinning gust of wind.

"On second thought captain—why don't we admit we're both stubborn bastards and start this shootout already."

The seven ship fleet zoomed towards me right into my tidal wave of status cure.

"Keep spinning you guys," I shouted to Chip and the phoenix.

The elemental spirit smiled, unphased by the sheer amount of violent force heading our way. "Sure Clay! Anything you want!"

I hoped this plan of mine worked. Otherwise we were screwed. I kept casting status cure over and over, feeding the glowing vapor sky more and more residual status cure spell. The patch of sky we were spinning around had become my cauldron. The incoming ships were my final ingredient.

The Arethkarian ships headed straight for us. "Duck!"

The gryphon made a sharp decline into the air, Chip and the Phoenix following straight behind us. Above, the Arethkarian ships flew right into our floating cloud of status cure.

There was an immediate tremor of air from the ships above us.

Gryph flew back up around the ships and I grinned at the sight. Shadow wraiths were losing their inky smoke exteriors. The pale players beneath were sad shells of humanity. Prisoners seeing the light of day after weeks of torture. With the status cure air keeping the debuff deactivated, they ripped off their slave necklaces and attacked the Arethkarian guards, soldiers, and crew in an animalistic fury.

The enemy ships were imploding from the inside.

This was Serena's other way.

I don't know why I didn't see it earlier. We didn't want to harm the enslaved Chosen; ultimately they were on our side. The key to winning was in saving the most amount of lives possible; not just the ones on our team.

In the distance the *Horizon's Dream* maneuvered through the air, circling the Arethkarian ships, unleashing loads of cannon fire and turret blasts. The battle was in our favor now. We were gloriously on the offensive while Arethkar's fleet was struggling to fight on two different fronts: on board their ships and outside of it.

"Okay, Gryph, land me down on the central ship there. That's Kaige's ship."

The gryphon soared upward, shooting through clouds and then back down in the air towards the deck of the large metallic dreadnought.

The deck was a bloodbath. The pale bald headed Chosen were enacting their vengeance on everything on board. The soldiers and crew had been so caught off guard by the player's sudden freedom from the enslaved buff, they weren't ready for the attack. Bodies of crewman laid strewn across the deck. Crowds of freed players were mauling the guards, stealing their weapons and shooting them.

A group of them ran at me when I landed.

"Don't shoot," I said. "I'm on your side. I'm a player too. I'm the one who cast the spell that freed you."

"Took you long enough," hissed one of the men. His eyes

were red and his veins were purple along his paper white skin.

"I'm sorry," I said. "You're right, but there's still more of you out there, so we can't give up now."

The antagonistic man growled. I understood where he was coming from. I understood the anger boiling inside of him. When you were this angry, you weren't trying to make sense or have a rational argument or discussion, there was only one thing you wanted to communicate: rage.

Luckily, two other wearied and newly freed Chosen stepped between me and the angry man.

"He's right," he said. "We're free of the necklaces but we're not free of this ship. We've been given an opportunity here. Let's not squander it."

The man turned around and nodded his head to me. "What do you need from us?"

"Keep doing what you're doing," I said. "Take over these ships. Let's get them in our control."

"Done," said the angry man, smashing a clenched fist into his palm. He ran off down the deck, picking up two mana rifles off fallen soldiers on the way.

"I'm looking for Oren Kaige," I said. "If we capture him, this battle is as good as over. Where on the deck is he?"

The two players pointed to a platform above us. It was a smaller deck hidden by a tinted glass wall. The Captain's Quarters.

I nodded my head. "Thanks."

I ran up the deck towards a staircase, stepping over fallen bodies. The ship was pure chaos. The slaves were rebelling, a mutiny aboard the ship. I had to duck behind a wall to avoid a blast of a laser turret the slaves had commandeered.

I hurried out once the coast was clear and up the steps to

the upper deck. Smoke filled the sky. Dotted across the clouds were other Arethkarian ships rocking in the wind. The enslaved Chosen were overthrowing the enemy command.

The *Horizon's Dream* was no longer firing now that they saw what was happening on board. Instead they were taking refugees, those injured and not strong enough to fight. Good work guys.

On the upper deck, I ran to the captain quarters and kicked down the door.

"It's over Kaige," I yelled. "Your fleet is no longer at your control."

No one responded.

It was empty.

A muffling came from the crystal transmitter. I pulled it out of my pocket and heard Shade on the other end.

"Captain, we gotta problem."

Emerging from the clouds was the sky fortress, La-Archanum. Guns and cannons ready to take us out.

35

"Pretty castle!" said Chip floating beside me.

"Crap," I said. "That doesn't look good."

The Arethkarian flag flapped from the top pole at the highest summit of the floating city. There was my explanation for why Oren Kaige wasn't here on the ship. He'd taken over La-Archanum.

The battle just got a whole lot more complicated. I ran back down the deck and found the two players who'd helped me earlier. They were crouching down, tending to the wounded.

"You guys are the two most level-headed people on this ship right now. When you're done taking out the guards, I want you to head to the captain's quarters and man this ship. Get in communication with the others. I suspect all the Arethkarian's on board are either getting killed, thrown overboard, or imprisoned."

The two men shook their heads. "None will be taken prisoner. They will all die."

"Fair," I said. "I have to go deal with the rest of them on board the sky fortress. So I'm leaving the rest to you."

The two men nodded. Their eyes were hollowed out with sadness and despair. Yet talking to them, making a plan, they had the faintest glimmer of hope. This violent blood-soaked battle was the end to the nightmare they'd been living through.

I walked away from them and called to Gryph circling the ship above.

Coming, human friend.

Gryph flew down and I got on his back once more and flew towards the *Horizon's Dream*.

"Your plan worked Clay!" said Serena as I landed back on board. "You freaking did it. You found another way."

The ship was still operating in frantic battle mode. Jackson was behind the wheel, dictating orders to the crew. Shade and Kari were tending to the wounded and newly freed Arethkarian players at the side of the ship. They escorted those in good enough shape down below the deck where it was safer.

"We got a new problem though," I said.

Serena's smile disappeared and she nodded solemnly, turning towards the floating metal fortress in the sky.

A ship came zooming towards us from outside one of the lower hatches. It was a non-Arethkarian build, wooden with Aeri engravings similar to our ship.

"Hold fire," I said. "But be ready."

The ship got bigger and bigger until it was right near us and swerved to the side. Walking across the deck was the pirate queen Bella.

"Go on and say it," said the Lirana captain, looking down at me, tipping her hat. "You told me so."

I shrugged. "They didn't hold their end of the bargain?"

"I was a fool," said the pirate captain. "I thought I was doing what was best for my citizens. I was wrong. Now I know what I have to do: bloody take back my city and save my people!"

"Sounds like a big job Bella," said Shade. "You wanna let us help you out?"

"Why do you think I'm bloody here, now come on and follow me."

"But what about the rest of 'em," said Jackson, pointing to the chaos and carnage happening on board the Arethkarian fleet.

He was right. We were in a bind. I didn't want to leave the newly freed players to fend for themselves, even if they were doing a pretty good job of it so far. Neither did I want to split the party, but we didn't have many other options.

"Why don't you go on board Bella's ship," said Jackson, "And I'll man *Horizon's Dream* and look after these people."

The man stared at me. He wasn't making a suggestion; this is what he wanted to do.

"Let me do them the favor you did me," said the brawler.

I nodded my head. "My pleasure Jackson. Your fists will be missed in the upcoming battle."

The helmsman grinned. "Oh you don't have to tell me —*I know*."

Bella threw down a plank between our ships. "Come on over, we've got a floating city to siege."

Shade, Serena, and Kari ran on board first. I came next. Chip floated beside me. "Field trip to the pretty floating castle!"

Bella shuddered at the spirit. "I see you made a new friend. New class too. Well done."

"Thanks," I said. "But enough small talk. Take us to La-Archanum and show us where Kaige is hiding."

The pirate captain tipped her hat and wagged her tail. "Alright, let's go."

The ship flew through the sky approaching La-Archanum. It landed at a small loading bay near the bottom.

"We'll have to work our way back to the top," said Bella. "Kaige has soldiers on every level. He knows we'll be coming for him."

"We better get started then," I said.

"Yippee! Big battle," said Chip.

"Seriously, is this guy some kind of sociopath," said Serena. "Why's he so happy? We're risking our lives here?"

"I'm immaterial!" cheered Chip.

"I think he's chilled out to the fact that he's an immaterial spirit," said Shade. "He's got nothing to worry about. He's pretty much dead already. He's a sprite. Just chilling. I dig it. It makes me want to be immaterial."

"Bad idea. If you were immaterial," mused Bella. "I couldn't stab you in the back."

"My thoughts exactly," said Shade.

We disembarked the ship and Bella marched forward to a nearby elevator, leading the way. She spun around on her feet. "Alright lads and—" She looked to Chip. "Overly enthusiastic spirit thing. This elevator will take you to the engine core at the center of La-Archanum. You'll have to fight your way across the hall. I'm sure he's stationed soldiers on the way to the control room. I'm sure he'll be hiding there."

"You're coming with us, no?" said Serena.

"I wish love," said the pirate queen. "But my city's been hijacked, I gotta go protect my citizens on the ground. Now stop wasting time here chatting to me and go."

We all nodded our heads and entered the elevator. As the lift took us higher and higher up the floors of the sky city, the blue sky and clouds rushed past us from the glass windows. Kari lifted her staff and hands, casting strength and defensive buffs onto each of us. Shade kept both his hands near his waist, ready to pull out whichever weapon was necessary for when the elevator door opened. Serena gripped her massive blade. I kept my spell casting hands and arms loose.

"This is so intense," said Chip. "I've never felt so alive. Or wait: are spirits even alive?"

"Don't look at me," I said. "Beyond what you've told me, I don't know shit about spirits."

Chip was about to reply when the elevator doors opened and a burst of gun fire greeted us. We all jumped to the sides to avoid the blast.

Serena jumped in front and held up her sword horizontally. The bullets knocked into her blade as she walked forward. We all followed behind her.

Two soldiers fired at us from the end of the hall. With their bullets quickly losing their effectiveness against Serena's sword shield, ash and debris flicking off the blade as we marched forward.

One guard pulled out a rudimentary grenade from his waist and lifted up his arm ready to toss it in our direction.

"Cover!"

But the soldier didn't throw the grenade. Rather blood burst out from behind his neck, his face pale, his eyes bulging in shock. He fell over, revealing Shade behind him with crimson drenched daggers.

+148 EXP!

Shade disappeared in a flash, sliding behind the other soldier and knocking him to the ground. Serena dropped her sword shield stance and charged the soldier. First Shade tripped him and made him stumble on his feet. Disoriented the soldier looked up to face the front of Serena's incoming crushing blow. The dead soldier fell to the floor and a burst of experience points rushed past my HUD.

"Good job guys," I said. "Kaige awaits us beyond here. Remember, he's using the power of corrupted fragments. His abilities will be deadly. For all of us."

Serena and Kari nodded. They understood what I was saying. We were entering a battle with permadeath on the cards.

Shade was bent over the soldiers, searching their fallen bodies for loot. He checked their hands for rings, underneath their plate armor for necklaces, and their pockets for gold. He stood up satisfied with new finds and looked up at us.

"Did you hear what I just said?"

"Final fight, permadeath, yada yada," said Shade. "You know, for some of us, your so-called 'permadeath' is our everyday life."

"Sorry," I said. "You're not about to switch teams on us?"

"For these fools," said Shade. "Not a chance. We ready to roll?"

"Hell yeah," I said.

We moved down the hall and reached a giant sliding door. There was a glowing orb at the side.

"I guess doorknobs are no longer in fashion," said Serena. "Hello, magitech chic."

She pressed the glowing orb and the door in front of us slid open. I expected an onslaught of bullet fire and war cries to follow, but instead we got an unsettling quiet, with murmurs in the distance. The new room was incredibly large. Much bigger than I had expected. To the left was a curved glass window circling the entire chamber. We crept into the room, making sure to stay hidden in the shadows of the pillars and sides of the room.

"It's seven against one," said a voice which I instantly recognized as Oren Kaige's. "Why aren't our ships doing anything?"

"We've lost contact with them sir," said another voice. "No one is responding to our communication crystals."

A flicker of a radio signal echoed across the room.

"What's this?"

"...we're coming for you, you bastards..."

Oren Kaige whipped the communication crystal, smashing it against the wall.

"Ready the cannon," said Kaige. "We'll destroy our own fleet if we have to."

We stepped into the large captain's area and found Oren Kaige and two soldiers, overlooking the battle in the skies.

"Don't you dare hurt those ships," I said. "Oren Kaige— I'm putting you under arrest for war crimes against Laergard."

The Arethkarian general laughed in my face. "It's funny to hear your enemy's thoughts, don't you think? You see me as the bad guy, yet when I look at you: I see the death of my family, my people, my whole civilization."

"Save it," said Serena. "Tyrants always rationalize their bullshit."

"So be it," said the captain. "I'll die before I give myself up to you."

"Then bring it," I yelled, conjuring a ball of flame between my fingers and whipping it at the deranged-looking man.

He lifted up his claw pincer and blocked the attack.

"Pff," he said. "Your petty attacks won't do anything against me and my power."

He directed his pincer arm at me and it stretched out towards us, his arm becoming a veiny fleshy demonic pole of destruction.

"Everybody duck," I yelled. We jumped to the sides. I smacked onto the floor and rolled, dodging the incoming bullets.

"Take out the little guys first," I said.

"Aye aye captain," yelled Chip, swerving through the air and spinning around one of the soldiers. His speed caught the soldier off guard. Disoriented, the Arethkarian shot at Chip, but he flew through the bullets. The spirit laughed, shouting. "Sorry you can't hit me. I'M IMMATERIAL!"

Chip unleashed an energy blast and the soldier toppled backwards. Shade—always at the right place at the right time—was directly behind the disoriented soldier with two dagger stabs in the spine.

Serena was across the chamber, duking it out with the other soldier while dodging the sweeping destruction of Oren Kaige. She kicked the soldier in the gut, then lifted her sword and pressed it into him for the finishing move.

Now it was us versus Kaige.

I lifted my arm, readying my Prophetic Seal power. It was time to remove our handicap. De-scale Kaige's power of the corrupted fragments.

Let's go.

Kaige smiled and directed his stretchy pincer claw towards me.

"Clay, watch out!"

Shade tackled me away from the attack, the demonic arm missing both of us.

Serena charged him ready to duel him one on one.

"Guys don't get too close," I yelled. "He's too powerful in his current form."

"Shut up hero boy," said Serena, between grunts and slashes of her sword; steel versus corrupted crab claws. "Ever hear of a distraction?"

She was right. Now was the perfect chance to hit him with the Prophetic Seal spell. I readied my arm and selected, "*//run: remove_corrupted_file*". A black blast shot across the room and smashed right into Oren Kaige.

His whole person flickered and fragmented. His crab arm disappeared, the lines on his contorted monstrous face relaxed and smoothed into a much more human looking visage.

The man gasped, shocked by his loss of power, by his return to normal Haeren form. He didn't spend too much time distressed though. His first action was unsheathing his sword and stabbing Serena in the stomach. He wrenched the sword into her flesh and dragged it out and stabbed her again. With his other hand he pulled out a knife and dug it straight into her neck.

Serena's whole body went pale. First with shock, then with lifelessness.

A Party Member Has Fallen

"SERENA!" yelled Kari, shooting a healing blast her way.

I stood there speechless. It was too late. She wasn't coming back to see the end of this fight. What world would she respawn too? One where we'd won or a world where we'd lost? Her fate—along with the rest of ours—was in our hands now, hanging in the balance of this battle.

Oren Kaige grinned. "You think I was some kind of weakling before I was empowered with forbidden magic? I was chosen for such power for a reason."

He moved with intense speed and stabbed Kari. The little fox girl went pale with shock.

A Party Member Has Fallen

"Shade stay close to me," I said. "We need a plan to finish this guy."

"Don't worry Clay I got this!" yelled Chip, zooming through the air towards the general.

Kaige laughed, lifting up his hand and unleashing an energy blast and shattering the spirit into dust.

A message rolled across my HUD.

Chip (Bound Spirit Level 1) has fallen. He cannot be summoned for another 7:59:00 minute(s).

It was me and Shade now against this psychopath.

"Remember the time we were caught in the arena pits?" said Shade.

"Yeah—it was a perfectly avoidable situation but someone cheated at cards."

"You have your perspective and I have mine," said Shade. "But the main thing was: we were caught in a hard situation and we fought our way out. We can do it here again."

"Definitely," I said. "We need to slow him down."

I shot out a lightning cage spell at his leg, but the warrior dodged it. He rushed towards us and I created a flame wall. He turned right. I frosted the floor he was moving towards and the general slipped and fell onto the ice. He got up and moved at a slower pace across the ice field.

Now was our chance.

Shade went one way while I faced the warrior head on. I conjured iceblade as I ran towards the enemy captain. The frozen hilt of ice formed in my hands as I charged the captain.

"A magic user against a trained swordsman," balked Kaige, meeting my slash of my ice sword with his own silver blade.

Our swords locked and clashed into a battle of strength. I swung in my other hand at Kaige, my fingers crackling with electric energy. I aimed straight for his head. Kaige jerked and hesitated. It was a lose-lose situation for him. Block my skull shock and my sword attack went through; don't block it and, well, receive free electroshock therapy.

He lifted his sword to block my magic attack, making his decision. I swiped my ice sword across, puncturing his waist armor and landing another chilled buff stacked against the other. His movements were slowed.

Kaige screamed in pain and rage. "This isn't happening!"

"Oh yes it is," I grinned.

Shade appeared from behind with his daggers drawn. He stabbed them into the Kaige's back.

+critical hit!
+critical hit!
+critical hit!

Kaige fell onto his knees, blood dripping from his mouth and covering his teeth.

"You've won Chosen," he said. "I hope you don't destroy this world and the people who inhabited it before you came."

"That was never our intention. We aren't these evil beings you've painted us out to be."

"I know not all you Chosen are evil, but do you really believe standing in my shoes or his—" He glanced over to Shade. "That we can trust you to treat us equally and fairly. You live a life without death or punishment. Like living gods while we suffer the consequences saved only for mortals."

I wanted to tell him he wasn't wrong in the way he felt: we had an uphill battle to climb, one requiring all of us to trust one another and offer a hand of peace. Only then will we create a world where the NPCs and Chosen lived side by side. I wanted to tell him all this, but before I even opened my mouth, he took the hilt of the sword in his chest and stabbed it deeper into his body.

Experience points rushed across my HUD but I closed my eyes and ignored them; I didn't wish to measure a person's life in the number they gave me towards my next level.

36

Fireworks spread across the skyline of Land's Shield. The whole city was alive with celebration, following the signing of the peace treaty between Arethkar and Laergard. The hostile nation had turned around its remaining ships and was returning to its own sky shores. The trade blockades were removed and goods were flowing freely between the different continents and nations once again. Peace—however transient and temporary it may have felt—had returned to Illyria for the time being.

The freed Arethkarian players from the fleet had been given lodging in an empty soldier's barracks near the keep and were being looked after with food and clothing. They were hollowed out and exhausted. They had a lot to take in before any semblance of normality would return to their lives.

I had finished checking on them and returned to the keep where the king and officers were holding a celebration to the end of the war.

Drinks were passed around. Officers chatted with each other nicely. Shade was wearing a fancy tuxedo and Kari wore a pretty purple dress. Serena wore a stunning red gown with a sexy side slit, revealing her toned leg and thigh.

"Like what you see?" asked Serena. She beamed me a wicked smile and stared right at me with her bright blue eyes.

I didn't have a chance to screw up the moment by saying something idiotic because the king rose at the front of the party. He was about to give a speech.

"We have much to celebrate tonight," he said. "Our enemy has retreated from a fight with us. An impending war has been squashed. Everyone from our scientists to our soldiers have helped us achieve this goal; but, without the help of one group of individuals, we wouldn't be here today. For that group—the mischievous Shade, the caring Kari, the bold and strong Serena, the brave Jackson, and their wizened leader Clay—are to be honored this evening."

A servant came up behind the king holding a box of items.

"To Shade," the king said. "I present you these two shadow daggers."

The king took two dark obsidian daggers and handed them to the thief.

"To Kari," continued the king. "I offer this staff of holy healing."

He handed her an incredible silver magic staff with powerful etchings and runes.

"To Serena," said the king. "I present this grand blade."

He pulled out a massive blade soldier's sword with a golden hilt with emerald runes.

"To Jackson," he said. "I present to you these bracers."

He pulled out a beautiful pair of bracers, perfect for the brawler class.

"To Clay," said the king, turning to me last. "Who has

chosen a new path of magic with his summoner class. I grant you a plot of land in the city where you can store and care for your bound creatures and nurture them to become even more powerful and fight on your and hopefully Laergard's behalf."

The king nodded and smiled at me.

"And—" said the king. "Let us not forget the crew who helped them travel across the treacherous skies of Argon's Rage. They, too, deserve compensation. For every member aboard the *Horizon's Dream*, they'll see a payment of 5,000 gold coins and a barrel of the keep's finest wine!"

The whole room erupted with cheers and claps of celebration.

~

THE NIGHT soon turned to easier and more relaxed matters: drinking and dancing. A group of musicians played a slow tune and Serena and I swayed to the music together.

"All's well that end's well," smiled Serena.

I smiled back, but she saw right through me.

"Can't you be happy just for this evening, Clay," she frowned.

"I want to," I said. "But you and I both know this peace cannot last. There's still all those players on the Arethkarian continent, enslaved. We have to save them."

"I agree," she said. "But we're currently not strong enough for an invasion. We need to level up, get stronger, form allies. There's a lot to be done."

"You're right," I said. "And none of it can get done this evening. So let's celebrate how much we've gained so far."

"Exactly," smiled Serena, planting a kiss on my lips.

I kissed back but her lips were cold. I pulled my face

away and saw the whole room had frozen. Everyone across the party was paused in midstep.

Across the dance floor was Betina, guardian of dreams.

"A moment of utter bliss, a kiss of a loved one, lost in the embrace," said the girl. "In a moment such as that, people dream."

"This is barely a dream," I said. "I think I preferred it when you actually showed up there."

"I won't be keeping you," said the ghostly girl walking up to me. "I wanted to come and present my own congratulations to you for a job well done."

"Thanks, I guess."

She smiled and nodded.

"I can tell," she said. "You don't think this war with Arethkar is over."

"How can it be?"

"I'm glad you feel this way," said the girl. "But I must warn you. Oren Kaige had the power of the corrupted fragments yet still remained conscious. There is only one explanation for this. There are other guardians—brothers, sisters, and family of mine—that are working with Arethkar."

My stomach dropped. This didn't sound good.

"You're not just fighting a powerful nation Clay," said the girl. "You're now at war with the gods."

To be continued in A.K.O. Book 4!

Thank you so much for reading.

Get a FREE A.K.O. story by signing up to my mailing list.
Click the link or image below to get your FREE ebook short
story!

http://eepurl.com/dBOgOn

Author's Note

Thank you for reading my book from start to finish! I hope you enjoyed Clay's further adventures in book 3 of Arcane Kingdom Online. If you did, please consider leaving a review. As an indie author, reviews go a long way to achieving success, so please leave one if you can!

Thanks again for reading and see you soon!
-Jakob Tanner
www.jakobtanner.com

Join The Chosen (Jakob Tanner's Reading Group) on Facebook today!

If you're looking to connect with other fans of A.K.O. and want to stay up to date with all my book news, join the Arcane Kingdom Online facebook group here.

Need More Good Books?

Looking for something great to read while you wait for book 4 of A.K.O.? Let me recommend a few of my favorites!

If you're looking for more action-packed page-turning LitRPG goodness, look no further than M.H. Johnson's *Endless Online* series. I love this particular series due to its intergalactic sci-fi elements which we don't see enough of in this genre!

Another favorite of mine is Harmon Cooper's *Feedback Loop*. Cooper is a very humorous writer who manages to combine hardboiled detectives, snarky jokes, and virtual reality all into one awesome reading experience.

Crystal Shards Online by Rick Scott is another amazing series with a game world full of intrigue and characters you fall in love with.

The Hall by Frank Albelo is a great start to a promising new fantasy LitRPG series with a really unique and cool magic system.

I hope you enjoy!

Join the LitRPG Group on Facebook!

To learn more about LitRPG, talk to authors including myself, and just have an awesome time, please join the LitRPG Group.

Join the GameLit Society for more GameLit and LitRPG!

If you want to hang out with other GameLit fans and authors, consider joining the GameLit Society Facebook group here.

More LitRPG/GameLit Groups

If you're looking for more places to chat about LitRPG and GameLit, consider joining these facebook groups and forums as well.

LitRPG Books (Facebook Group)

LitRPG Forum (Facebook Group)

r/LitRPG (LitRPG Subreddit)